THE RULES OF

Gentility

By Janet Mullany

THE RULES OF GENTILITY

THE RULES OF

Gentility

JANET MULLANY

AVON

An Imprint of HarperCollinsPublishers

HarperCollins books may be purchased for educational, business, or sales promotional use. For information please write: Special Markets Department, HarperCollins Publishers, 10 East 53rd Street, New York, NY 10022.

FIRST EDITION

Interior text designed by Diahann Sturge

Library of Congress Cataloging-in-Publication Data
  Mullany, Janet.
    The rules of gentility / Janet Mullany.—1st. ed.
      p. cm.
    ISBN: 978-0-06-122983-1
    ISBN-10: 0-06-122983-0
    1. Young women—England—London—Fiction. 2. Mate selection—Fiction.
  I. Title.

PR6113.U43R85 2007
823'.92—dc22   2007012684

07 08 09 10 11   ov/RRD   10 9 8 7 6 5 4 3 2 1

To Alison Hill—
Chickiebaby, this one's for you.
With love, yo mama.

Acknowledgments

Many thanks to:

My fearless agent Lucienne Diver and my intrepid editor May Chen; the members of the Wet Noodle Posse, particularly Colleen Gleason, Delle Jacobs, and Lorelle Marinello, who encouraged me to go on with "that Regency chick"; my critique group The Tarts; Kathy Caskie and Kasey Michaels; writer friends Sammi Hoard, Randy Jeanne, Adrienne Regard, Pam Rosenthal, Robin L. Rotham, and Brooke Wills; the ladies of the Risky Regencies Blog and The Beau Monde; Rosie Mullany (and the rest of the Mullany gang), Gail Orgelfinger, and Maureen Sarson for digital and in person nice cups of tea, friendship, and support; and Steve—my editor made me take out the stuff about the Normandy Beach landings, so it's okay if you don't want to read this one.

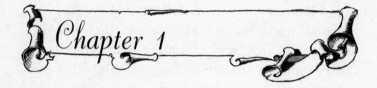

Chapter 1

Miss Philomena Wellesley-Clegg

It is a truth universally acknowledged that a single woman of fortune and passable good looks amuses herself in London with fashion, philanthropic works, and flirtation, until a suitable gentleman makes an offer. I consider the pursuit of the bonnets and a husband fairly alike—I do not want to acquire an item that will wear out, or bore me after a brief acquaintance, and we must suit each other very well. And although I have several gentlemen who have expressed an interest, I find all of them lack a certain something; and of course, with a gentleman you cannot replace the trim from another to make the perfect object, as tempting a thought as that might be, although indeed it would be an interesting experiment.

My current list of Possible Husbands is as follows:

1. Lord Elmhurst. Oh, he is the catch of the season. All we young ladies adore him. He is tall, handsome, rich, and charming, and danced twice with me at Lady Bellingham's the other night, complimented me on my headdress, and took me in to supper. The rumor is that he wishes for a wife whose pedigree will match his, but I wonder . . .

2. Viscount Elverton, who Mama says is a Catch, and she expects him to make an offer any day. Must I face a lifetime of listening to Elverton talk about his dogs and horses? Will he refer to me as a fine bitch who breeds like clockwork, or a mare with a capital gait?

3. The Mad Poet, although I am not sure he writes poetry, or at least gets much beyond the first line, of which he seems to have many. He is excessively handsome. It is such a shame his real name is Mr. Hengest Carrotte.

4. Dear Mr. Thomas Darrowby does not have a penny to his name, although I think he would do well enough. He is rather like the bonnet you keep hanging by the door and put on

when you do not have the time to ponder over the collection and must leave in a hurry. And it is a pity, for of all the gentlemen I know, he is the most affable, and Mama and Papa like him, for he is my brother Robert's best friend.

5. Lord Aylesworth, who is the only gentleman I know who truly appreciates bonnets and has an excellent eye for trims and the line of a gown. He also enjoys gossip and the theater, and is always most elegant.

As I step from the hackney, I muse that I shall discuss the inventory with my dearest friend Julia, or Lady Terrant as I must now think of her. I have decided to send my maid home, and so that is how I find myself outside the Terrants' house, juggling three hatboxes and some other purchases, and looking around for a footman to help me. I am most anxious to show Julia what I have bought and see what she thinks of taking the silk flowers from the red velvet and replacing them with the new yellow ribbon, something that seemed like a good idea at the time, although now I have severe doubts.

Another hackney draws up, splashing a little mud on my skirts, and a servant emerges, even more laden down with boxes and baskets than I. He glances toward the Terrants' house, and then starts a lively conversation with the driver. I am quite surprised that Terrant, for I presume it is his doing, should pass down such a wretched coat to one of his servants—the man's collar is frayed, one elbow is out, and he wears a straw hat, even though it is barely spring. Obviously, he has traveled from the country, from one of their estates, as the brace of dead hares under one arm attests.

The front door of the house opens, and Julia runs down the steps. Why, she must have seen me arrive! How thoughtful she is.

One of my precious hatboxes falls from under my arm and rolls onto the pavement, and in trying to rescue it I let go of the rest. "You may take these inside with your other boxes," I say to the servant, and deposit my remaining possessions on top of the large trunk he has hauled out of the carriage, along with various other packages and baskets. One of them makes a loud, quacking sound, and I see he has brought a couple of ducks in a wicker cage.

"I—oh, why, certainly, miss." He doesn't sound very respectful although he does remove his hat. He needs a haircut—his mop of black hair curls over his collar, and, oh, shocking! When did he last shave?

"Inigo, my dear!" Julia runs to the servant and kisses his cheek, to my very great surprise. "You rascal, sir, you should have let us know to expect you. Why did you bring us ducks?" She bends down to stroke their feathers. "Oh, surely we shan't eat them. Look how pretty they are!"

"I wasn't intending you should. I thought the kitchen might keep them for their eggs. You look well, my love. I hope my brother treats you well." He gives her a smacking kiss on the cheek, his arm around her waist. "Lend me a shilling for the driver, there's a good girl. I'm somewhat low in the water."

Oh, I am mortified! So this is Inigo Linsley, Terrant's younger brother—the wicked one who so frequently cools his heels in the country. And I thought he was a servant!

Julia hands the driver a shilling she borrows from the butler. "Inigo, this is my dearest friend, Miss Philomena Wellesley-Clegg."

He has the brightest blue eyes and he bows as though we were introduced in a drawing-room and not on the street. "Ah. *Those* Wellesleys?"

"Oh, no, I don't believe so. We Wellesleys are from Lancashire, and my great-great-great-grandmother Hallelujah Clegg married into the family. She had a coal mine as a dowry."

"A coal mine? And Hallelujah? That's an interesting name."

"Yes, sir. She belonged to a devout nonconformist sect." I have found it best to be quite open about the source of my family's wealth; we have always been aware of it, as the mining of the coal seam that lies under our house causes it to sag most alarmingly. And I am so dreadfully tired of people always asking us if we are related to the Duke of Wellington (for we share the same surname), and then looking disappointed or contemptuous when I tell them we are not. Mr. Inigo Linsley, to his credit, looks only amused.

He is most handsome, or at least would be so when shaved and tidied up.

Servants have now appeared to gather up our respective parcels, and Julia gives instructions on their destinations—the hares, ducks, a leather bucket of live trout, and a large basket of lettuce and other greenstuffs go down the outside steps to the kitchen.

"Terrant did not tell me we had the pleasure of a visitor," Mr. Linsley says to me.

"A visitor? Oh, no. I have only been shopping for a few things."

He pokes a hatbox with one foot, clad in an extremely scuffed and unpolished boot. "Three bonnets? You only have one head, do you not? I thought you were moving in with your worldly goods."

"I am extremely interested in bonnets, and I assure you I have many more at home." I add, "I am considered something of an expert in the subject. Of course, I would not expect a gentleman to understand."

"Inigo, the Dowager Countess will have the vapors if she sees you looking like a scarecrow," Julia says. "Shame on you, wearing your country rags into town, but I am so glad you are here. Your mama and I are exceedingly vexed writing Terrant's speeches."

He makes a face. "So it's my turn. I should have known. Well, I'd best go and pay my respects to my mother and Terrant." He does not sound overjoyed at the prospect. Then he grins. He bends to pick something from the stone flags. "I believe this is yours, Miss Wellesley-Clegg."

Oh, heavens. It is a stocking, fallen from one of my parcels. I snatch it from him, my face heating up.

"I assure you, madam, my thoughts were far above it." He bows and ushers us into the house ahead of him, and by the time I realize what he has just said, Julia has taken my arm and led me upstairs to her private sitting room for serious talk about good works and bonnets.

Mr. Inigo Linsley

It is a strange phenomenon that as much as I look forward to visiting my family in town, once I am there we do nothing but drive each other mad.

Take my arrival, for instance, and that exceedingly silly girl.

I suppose Julia will expect me to squire her around until she giggles her way into a suitable match.

She has good taste in clocked stockings, however.

So musing, I pause at the drawing-room door, where a stranger stands contemplating the painting of my mother, the Dowager Countess, that hangs over the mantelpiece. For a long time I could not reconcile the woman in the painting with the female dragon I encountered while growing up—a strong-minded woman who would slash her way through the rose beds like a cavalryman and truss up any perennial feebleminded enough to droop in her presence. The woman in the painting wears an extremely diaphanous gown that threatens to float away in the slightest breeze, and holds a garland aloft. More shockingly, and I must admit this makes me somewhat uncomfortable, she is barefooted, and shows a considerable amount of shapely ankle. This is my mama, after all. I can only imagine how she railed at the hapless painter while valuable minutes ticked away, and she longed to change back into the serviceable and many-pocketed print gown she wears for her gardening pursuits.

Of course, when I was growing up I only saw her in the summers, after a series of tutors thrashed some classics into me and handed me on to a series of schoolmasters with equally strong arms. I have no idea what she, and my late papa, got up to in town. I believe they ran with a fast set, but it is indecent to speculate.

But who the devil is this caller? One of Terrant's political friends, I suppose.

I debate whether I should change and shave first, before curiosity gets the better of me, and I step into the room.

The stranger seizes my hand. "Good God!" he exclaims. "You must be young Inigo."

Young Inigo? Who the devil is this man to address me so?

"I see you don't remember me. But how could you?" He pumps my hand up and down with manly vigor. "Well, well."

His hands are rough and his face is pleasant enough, square and weather-beaten, lines at his eyes. Soberly if well dressed, he must be a well-off farmer or sailor, at a guess. Certainly not a gentleman.

"Of course, you were still in petticoats," he continues.

I've had enough and withdraw my hand. "Insult me again, sir, and I shall demand satisfaction."

My mother enters the room, and stops dead when she sees the stranger. "Is it—it cannot be—"

In the short pause that follows where they both stare at each other, I step forward. "Do you know this fellow, madam?"

She ignores me. "Sev? Is it really you?"

"Admiral Septimus Riley, at your service, madam."

"Admiral!" She sinks onto a sofa, still gazing at him, while I, her prodigal son, wait for a word of welcome. I have little expectation of a fatted calf, for I did not bring one with me, although I might possibly partake of a jugged hare later.

"I was most saddened to hear of Harry," Admiral Riley, or Sev, or whatever his outlandish name is, says. And this is a clue that he is a true intimate of the family, for very few called my late father Harry. "I was in the Mediterranean at the time and did not hear the news until almost a year after."

"You wrote a very kind letter," my mother says, appearing almost benign as she does at the mention of the late earl. "It was a great comfort to me. And I remember how little Henry and George enjoyed that day you spent at our house, playing cricket with them."

"Aye, and you bowled me out," Admiral Sev says. "You had a fine, strong arm for a woman."

My mother played cricket with this man? A shocking thought, indeed. What did my father have to say?

She finally notices me. "Inigo, this is Admiral Riley, your father's second cousin. He visited us over twenty years ago—"

"Twenty-three years. You were too young to play cricket," the Admiral explains to me, "but you caused great excitement by eating a beetle."

"The Admiral was only a midshipman then," my mother adds. "You look like a beggar, Inigo. You should be ashamed. I believe Terrant wants to see you."

What! Leave my mother, a respectable widow, alone with this ruffian? "I was told he was out."

"Nonsense. He is in his study." She glares at me.

"A pleasure to have met you, Linsley." The Admiral is grinning all over his weather-beaten face. He wrings my hand again.

I am dismissed. As I make my way up the stairs, I think

again of Miss Wellesley-Clegg's stocking and wonder if the pretty embroidery matches an equally attractive ankle.

Miss Philomena Wellesley-Clegg

As Secretary of the Association for the Rescue and Succor of those in Extremis, which is to say, women who may be lured into vice and depravity, I am not terribly efficient today. Julia is the Lady President and we meet in the Terrants' most elegant drawing-room, where I am in swooning admiration of the marble panels that are not real marble at all; in fact, I have tested them with my thumbnail and found them to be paint, a most cunning deception.

Terrant passes through, guffaws most rudely when we tell him why we are gathered, and leaves for his club.

"It is too unfortunate," Julia says. "Every gentleman I know laughs when I tell him about our association, and it is a shame when you consider the good we do. Or at least intend to do, when we have our patron or patroness, for until then we have little influence. Philomena, please do pay attention. Miss Celia Blundell proposed that we have a concert both to raise funds for the Association and to attract patronage. It was seconded by Lady Amelia Hartwell, who has offered to play for us."

I dutifully record the motion. Although we do have money at our disposal between the four of us, it is as Julia says—we need patronage, preferably royal, for our Association to thrive. Although I am not sure a concert by Amelia is the answer, for her playing, although extremely correct, is, well, in a word, a great bore.

"Is there any discussion, ladies?"

"Um," I say. "It is only that . . . well, do you have any new pieces, Amelia?"

"I am always learning new pieces." Amelia looks slightly offended. "Music is my passion."

A man's voice interrupts our female gathering. "Ladies, why not invite a real musician?"

Lady Amelia Hartley bristles with indignation, and we all turn to look at this masculine invader, Terrant's younger brother Inigo, who leans against the doorway, one ankle crossed over another. He is astonishingly handsome, although once again, I regret to say, unshaven. I realize, to my dismay, that he wears the same breeches, and other clothes, of course, as he did at his brief appearance at Almack's last night. I wonder where he has been—in a gambling hell or some other pit of depravity? I feel quite wobbly and excited at the thought of it.

Julia frowns. "It is three o'clock in the afternoon, you sorry rake."

"I know of a singer who—"

"Certainly not, Inigo!" I am proud of Julia for her staunch support of our friend.

"And another thing . . ." He approaches our gathering, bows, and continues, "The name of your association is dreadful."

"No, it is not, Mr. Linsley," I say. "It is genteel. It mentions nothing indecent."

"You won't offer me a cup of tea? I am quite parched." He sinks onto the sofa next to me although we ladies have not invited him to sit.

His elbow brushes against mine.

Heavens! My pen drops a big blot of ink onto my yellow muslin.

"Oh, very well." Julia pours him a cup.

"But Mr. Linsley is right. It is a very cumbersome name," Miss Celia Blundell says as she reaches for more cake.

He winks at me. Why does Mr. Inigo Linsley have such pretty blue eyes, if somewhat bloodshot? "Call it the Protection of Innocent Maidens in Peril Society, Miss Wellesley-Clegg, and I'll give you a hundred guineas."

"You don't have a hundred guineas to offer anyone," Julia says. "Aren't you supposed to be helping Terrant write his speech?"

Mr. Linsley swipes the last piece of cake before Celia can get to it, which raises him in my estimation somewhat, for she is an accomplished eater. "I'd much rather stay here with you ladies. His speeches are excessively boring, even when I write them."

"Certainly not," Julia says. "If you wish to join our committee, you must make a contribution of fifty guineas, that you do not have, and you must take our work seriously."

"But, my dear Julia, I do. I long for you to rescue a fallen woman so I may succor her. I should like nothing better." He stands and bows. "Your servant, ladies. Oh, and I thought you'd like to know—Elmhurst is to be leg-shackled at last. He's engaged to Lady Caroline Bludge."

Celia, Amelia, and I digest this news with varying degrees of gloom and jealousy.

"I never thought she was very pretty," Julia says.

"Vulgar," Celia says, with her mouth full.

I find I don't really care. I am watching Mr. Linsley stroll to the door and sigh as it closes behind him. It is such a pity, as Mama says, that he is only a younger son and a wastrel, and I therefore cannot add him to my list.

I really must stop thinking about how he looks in his breeches.

I am in great need of distraction, and as every woman knows, a new bonnet is the best diversion of all. I must go shopping as soon as possible.

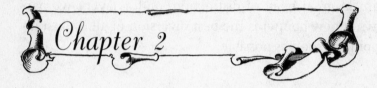

Chapter 2

Miss Philomena Wellesley-Clegg

One week later

"... And I do think it the most dreadful shame that Elmhurst has made an offer for Lady Bludge for she is not at all a pretty woman and a widow too and there have been rumors as I said to Mr. Wellesley-Clegg the other day our Philly for all her hair stands out like a great bush it is so distressing for it looked quite tidy when we left home and I know it is the fashion to look romantic but as I was saying Philly despite your hair you are prettier than she and you have a greater fortune and I thought he showed marked partiality and I fear people will say you are a flirt and chasing a title do we clap now or is there another movement I really cannot tell and although I know nothing of music . . ."

Oh, this is dreadful, just dreadful. My mother's whispered conversation is as relentless as Amelia's playing. Beside her my papa snores gently.

He is not alone. Half the room has fallen asleep, half of them are fidgeting or flirting, half wander in and out—and I know that does not add up, but the enormity, the horror, of Amelia's recital makes everything seem at least one and a half times worse than it is. Whether she has learned new pieces or not, the effect is the same—they all sound alike, and since she is always the first young lady, hardly bothering to attempt a show of modesty, to claw her way to the pianoforte at the slightest excuse, we have heard them, or something like them, a dozen times before. The Duke of R— snores openly, his mouth hanging open, and a thread of drool gathers on his chin and descends to his neckcloth. Will no one wipe off His Grace?

We are to serve supper after, so the greed of the *ton* traps them in our web of musical mediocrity. Meanwhile, across the room, Mr. Inigo Linsley fidgets until his mother, the Dowager Countess, smacks him on the hand with her fan. On her other side sits a gentleman I have met quite frequently in the last few days at the Terrants' house, Admiral Riley. As he releases a gentle snore, the Dowager Countess raps him with her fan, too, and he starts awake, saying something about the mainsail and those d—d Frenchies, *beg your pardon, ma'am.*

I catch Julia's eye and we giggle together in a helpless, childish way that will be impossible to stop if we look at each other.

"Mama," I whisper, "you are absolutely right. My hair is a fright. I shall go and do something about it."

I mean to ask Julia to accompany me, but she has turned to whisper something in Terrant's ear, their hands intertwined, and I do not have the heart to interrupt them. As I rise, I see Elverton's head swivel like a hound scenting a hare.

Oh horrors! If he catches me alone, he may propose.

I leave the room at a brisk pace and hesitate. I know the Terrants' house quite well, but when I emerge into an unfamiliar passageway, I do not know which way to turn. I am sure Elverton follows, so I take the first doorway I find and lean against the shut door while deciding what to do next.

And now he is pushing at the door, turning the handle as though he thinks it locked, or jammed. Another room opens from this one, I see, and I dart toward that doorway. At the same time, Elverton, or so I think it must be, pulls the door tightly closed, and there is a dreadful ripping sound. The train of my dress is caught in the door!

"What the d—l . . ." says the voice on the other side.

Oh, thank heaven. It is not Elverton. In fact, it is the only gentleman I should welcome under these circumstances.

"Aylesworth?" I grab the back of my gown with one hand and open the door. "In here immediately, if you please."

"I beg your pardon?"

"Now!" I grab his sleeve and haul him in, afraid that Elverton snoops around outside and may join us. "You must go and fetch me some pins."

He lounges against the door, raises his quizzing-glass, and examines me from head to toe. "Lord, Miss Wellesley-Clegg, you look quite a fright."

"Thank you, Aylesworth. The pins, if you please."

He sighs and reaches into the pocket of his immaculately tailored coat. Of course, if any man were to carry pins on his person, it would be Aylesworth. "A moment. You may have these on one condition."

"What is that? Not that I shall agree to anything, of course."

"Tell me, who is that fascinating creature next to the Dowager Countess of Terrant?"

That *what*? "Oh, that's Admiral Riley."

"Madam, credit me with some taste." He rolls his eyes. "The other one."

"But the Admiral is quite fascinating. He has some exciting stories of life at sea. I suppose you mean Mr. Inigo Linsley."

He drops one pin, dangled from his fingertips, onto the palm of my hand. "Indeed. One of Terrant's brothers, I presume?"

"Yes, the youngest. There is another one in the country who took orders."

"Indeed." He taps a pin thoughtfully against his teeth. "Quite the best-looking member of that family, although the young countess has some elegance. Whereas you, my dear—what on earth have you done to yourself?"

"I was wondering when you'd ask." I move over to a lamp on a small table and squint over my shoulder. I let out a loud cry of alarm, gather some detached fabric in my fist, and attempt to pin it into place.

"Dear, dear." Aylesworth moves to inspect the damage. "Don't be a cake, Miss Wellesley-Clegg. I assure you I have no designs on your honor. Hold still. Did you tack this together especially for the occasion?" He whistles softly through his teeth as he pleats and pins the back of my gown back into position. "Do not attempt any violent movements, Miss Wellesley-Clegg, and you shall survive the rigors of the evening. But—"

Someone else is coming into the room! Aylesworth and I look at each other with sudden understanding. If we are discovered together, with the cream of the *ton* here, he will be obliged to offer for me and I to accept him. While a gentleman who carries pins and is adept at making repairs to a lady's gown is most useful, I am not sure I wish to marry him for that reason alone.

He extinguishes the lamp, and we both duck behind a screen in one corner of the room. That, the table, and a sofa, are its only furniture, and the window shutters are still open, allowing a little light to come in from the gaslit street outside. My cream-colored gown and Aylesworth's oyster-gray satin coat and breeches will be highly visible in the dim light. We can only hope the intruder will not stay.

The other person—no, persons, there are two of them—blunder their way through the room. They do not seem particularly concerned with their surroundings, for they seem only intent on each other, breathing heavily, with much rustling and sighing.

Then one of them backs into the sofa, and I hear it creak as he or she sits on it.

"Wait," says a female voice.

"What's wrong, my dear?"

She sounds out of breath. "Can't bend in these d—d stays."

Heavens! I know who they are!

There are some soft, moist sounds—goodness, they are kissing!—and then a clatter as something falls onto the wooden floor. I suspect she must have removed the busk from her stays.

The rustles increase, as do the kissing sounds, and I listen in horrified fascination.

"Permission to come aboard, ma'am?"

"Aye, aye, Cap'n." She giggles.

Oh, this is dreadful! The Dowager Countess is known as one of the proudest ladies in London. And at her age, too! This is making me most uncomfortable, and I whisper into Aylesworth's ear, "We cannot stay here."

He nods, reaches for the lamp we so recently extinguished, and hurls it across the room.

The couple spring apart, with some colorful expressions that I suppose must be nautical terms on his part, and appear, in the half-dark, to be putting their clothing to rights. Then they stumble from the room, and thankfully, Aylesworth and I are alone.

"Well, well, well," he drawls. "And such a respectable lady, too. I am quite shocked. And so, my dear, we'd best return, but separately to preserve your reputation. After you, Miss Wellesley-Clegg."

"Thank you for pinning my gown."

"Your servant, madam. As a reward, I should be delighted to accompany you and your maid next time you visit the milliner's."

"I should be honored," I say, thinking that he might even

be quite useful, but at the same time resolving not to put the plan into practice.

As I step into the corridor, the door from the recital opens, and I see to my horror that I am once again on the verge of a compromising situation.

It is the Mad Poet, whose hair is in worse disarray than my own, although I suspect he spends time to make it so. "Madam—goddess—"

He falls to his knees. There is a loud, vulgar sound of the sort not often heard in polite society (except, according to my brother Robert, when the ladies withdraw after dinner and such sounds are in great evidence, and appreciated, nay, encouraged). Heavens, I hope he does not think it is me!

"D—n it!" He scrambles to his feet and regards the knees of his breeches.

The sound I just heard was in fact that of satin ripping. The knees of both breeches, which are fashionably tight (one cannot help but notice such things), are split across, and beneath them the poet wears rather pretty embroidered garters.

He shrugs, in acknowledgment of damage done, and drops to his knees again. "Have pity on me!"

"If you need pins, Mr. Carrotte, I believe Lord Aylesworth may have some."

"Pins! Oh, Miss Wellesley-Clegg, adored creature. I shall die for a smile. Feel how my heart pounds like a wounded creature!"

He grabs my hand and presses it to his waistcoat.

"Sir, release me! I shall be ruined if we are found here together."

"You have ruined me, Miss Wellesley-Clegg. The sun

is dark in my eyes, the beauties of nature itself appear as dross, because you will not favor me with a look, a smile. Cruel temptress!"

I attempt to tug my hand away, which he holds tight against his chest. "That's a very handsome waistcoat," I say in an attempt to placate him. "I like the embroidery. Please let me go, Mr. Carrotte."

"Fair cruelty, you will kill me. To talk of a gentleman's waistcoat at such a time! Have you no feelings, madam?"

"Of course I have feelings. It is just that I do not have them for you, sir, as I have made quite clear. Now let me go!" I aim a kick at his leg, and I regret that my aim is not very good, and in fact I kick him elsewhere (another interesting male phenomenon Robert has shared with me).

He gives a loud grunt, drops my hand, and doubles up, both hands in an indelicate place.

"I'm sorry," I say, for he appears to be in some pain, "but I did ask you . . ."

Aylesworth joins me in the corridor and looks aghast at the Mad Poet on the floor. "Good lord, Miss Wellesley-Clegg, must you have every man in London at your feet? Carrotte, may I be of some assistance?"

I am reluctant to stay with them and so retreat back into the room from which I so recently escaped. There is another lamp burning on the table, and a servant sweeps up the remains of the broken one. She curtsies to me and leaves. A small looking-glass on the wall shows me that my hair is indeed a dreadful fright as my mother said, and I should endeavor to repair it—how else will I explain my protracted absence?—I remove my gloves, spit on my hands, smooth down my hair, and replace a few pins.

And then . . . oh, no. Someone is opening the door. Really, this is just dreadful! Can I not get a moment's solitude? I do hope it is not the Poet—my brother did not tell me how long recovery from such an Incident takes, and while I do not wish him to be discovered in such an indelicate posture, neither do I want him to resume his pursuit.

So, foolishly, I retreat behind the screen.

A couple reel into the room, tightly clasped together.

To my horror, it is Mr. Inigo Linsley and Lady Caroline Bludge. She shoves—there is no delicate way to say this, either—him up against the wall, her hands clasping his coat. I am most impressed that they manage to do all this with their mouths locked together.

"D—n, we can't do this," Mr. Linsley says, when his mouth is free for a moment, for I imagine they must have to breathe. "I offered to take you into supper. You're engaged."

"One last time. Elmhurst won't mind. He won't know." She is breathless, and her bosom rises and falls so dramatically I wonder how it stays in her gown. "Why were you in the country so long? I have been mad for you. And you've been in town a week and not called on me."

"Caro, don't be foolish. I don't want Elmhurst to kill me." I notice that although he protests, he does not attempt to escape or let her go, and his voice lacks the conviction I would have thought appropriate. So he and Lady Caroline had a liaison! It is a pity Aylesworth is not with me, for he would appreciate this greatly, loving gossip as he does.

To my surprise, Lady Caroline drops to her knees in front of Inigo. Oh, poor woman, is she about to beg for his favors? I cannot countenance this!

"Sir!" I emerge from behind the screen. "You should be ashamed of yourself!"

Mr. Linsley says some rather interesting words—to be sure, my vocabulary is greatly expanded tonight—and Lady Caroline, whose hand is at the, well, in the vicinity of Mr. Linsley's breeches, utters a shriek and leaps to her feet.

"Oh! Miss Wellesley-Clegg! I was, er, looking for an earring!"

What sort of fool does she take me to be? Unless she has a hidden, third ear, there is no earring she could possibly have lost.

Mr. Linsley leans against the wall, arms folded, and regards us both with a smirk.

Lady Caroline hisses at me, "If you tell anyone of this, I shall ruin you. You should not even be in society, for you are from Trade and your family is excessively ill-bred for no lady would spy on another so—"

"Hold your tongue, Caroline!"

I think Mr. Linsley's response startles Lady Caroline almost as much as it does me, for she slaps his face, wrenches the door open, and leaves, slamming it behind her.

Mr. Linsley straightens his disordered neckcloth and bows.

Under the circumstances it is a ludicrous action, and I cannot help giggling.

"I regret you were, ah, exposed to such a scene," he says. "And Lady Caroline was inexcusably rude."

"It is no matter, sir." Well, what can I say? That my maidenly modesty is outraged? It was, in fact, rather interesting, and I am now not convinced that she was about to beg him for anything, as I first thought. I shall have to ask Julia, or my sister Diana, about it.

He nods, then steps past me to pick up something from the floor.

He grins and holds out the discarded busk. I suppose the servant did not pick it up while I was in the room, for she was intent only on sweeping up the broken lamp, and the busk lay half under the sofa. It is an exceedingly pretty one—I am quite envious—carved and painted ivory, and with the Terrant coat-of-arms prominently featured in the design.

He says, "Julia and Terrant should really be more discreet. You might have seen worse, Miss Wellesley-Clegg."

I almost did, and obviously he has no inkling whatsoever of it.

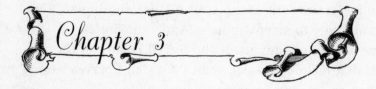

Chapter 3

Mr. Inigo Linsley

". . . And it is too bad," says my mother, "that those in Trade now fancy themselves the equals of the *ton*. In truth, I do not know what Julia was thinking of, to sponsor her in society." She frowns in the direction of Miss Wellesley-Clegg, who is on the opposite side of Bond Street with a woman who is probably her maid and several gentlemen in attendance.

Miss Wellesley-Clegg looks in our direction at that moment, recognizes the Dowager Countess, curtsies, and smiles. I could swear the sun comes out from behind the clouds and transforms the dingy environs of London into something clean and sparkling. I come to an abrupt halt and drop one of my mother's parcels.

A gentleman darts to our side and picks it up.

"Why, Sev, what a charming surprise," my mother says.

"Lady Terrant." He sweeps off his hat and bows. "How extraordinary to meet you here. And you, Linsley."

There is something about the forced civility of the moment that makes me suspicious. I am glad I persuaded my mother to let me accompany her—besides, Terrant has been more overbearing than usual, and I was glad to leave the house—although naturally she insisted she should go alone. Obviously the last thing she needs is the company of a garrulous old salt.

"Admiral Riley." I bow. "Lady Terrant was saying but a moment ago she wished to return home. Good day to you, sir."

"Nonsense. Give him that parcel, Sev. Inigo, you may return home. I have to see my dressmaker and Sev may escort me." She nods in the direction of Thomas Smith, Haberdashers to Gentlemen, where I am sure she never shops.

"But—"

Sev places the parcel on top of the precarious armful I already hold. "All ship-shape, Linsley? Capital, capital. I'll hail you a hackney."

"There's no need, sir." I edge toward my mother and mutter at her, "Madam, may I suggest you make your escape with me? Have you not had your fill of tales of derring-do on the high seas?"

"Don't be a fool." She turns her back on me and takes Sev's arm.

Good God, as though it is not enough to have the fellow in and out of our house the past week—why he must have dined with us three times at least and stayed to the bitter end of that hideous evening of pianoforte music two nights ago—she must subject herself to more punishment, and God knows why. I watch the two of them amble down Bond Street, arm in arm, zig-zagging slightly as though tacking in a tricky wind. The hackney seems to have slipped Sev's mind.

With some difficulty I manipulate my parcels—hers, rather—so most of them dangle from their twine loops on my left hand, with a couple tucked under my arm, and cross the street to see what Miss Wellesley-Clegg is about. She and her group are clustered around the doorway of Hooker's Circulating Library—that appalling molly Aylesworth, whom I know by sight (and that is quite enough), Carrotte the poet, and a stranger, a gentleman who stands next to her, laden with parcels (like myself and Miss Wellesley-Clegg's maid), gazing at her with adoration. It is this gentleman that Miss Wellesley-Clegg addresses as I approach.

"Now, Tom, I assure you there is no need to accompany me. Why, you must find shopping with a lady exceedingly tedious, and now I have some books, I shall return home."

Tom? Is she engaged to him?

To my surprise she graces me with another delightful smile. "Mr. Linsley, what a pleasant surprise. Do you know Mr. Tom Darrowby? He is from Lancashire, too, and almost like a brother to me. And Aylesworth and Mr. Carrotte, of course, you know."

Aylesworth gives me the sort of look that a month or so

ago, from Lady Caroline Bludge, would have led to highly indecent acts. However, I learned to deal tactfully with such fellows at school and bow slightly in his direction. Tom Darrowby looks most put out at the arrival of another gentleman to the party, and at his introduction as an honorary brother. If he is not yet engaged to Miss Wellesley-Clegg I suspect he should like to be. Carrotte, as befits the great poet he fancies himself to be, scribbles in a small notebook.

"Linsley," Aylesworth murmurs, eyeing me as though he has not had a square meal in weeks, "do persuade this lovely woman to allow us to accompany her into the hallowed ground of her milliner. Why, she is a cruel flirt. She has mentioned several times to me a certain bonnet she hungers for, and promised to ask my opinion on the matter."

"I have done so, sir," Miss Wellesley-Clegg replies. "I have described it in great detail, and I must think on the matter further. It is a serious business, my lord, and a decision a woman must make in an atmosphere of quiet contemplation. Mr. Linsley, you would not want to accompany a woman into a milliner's shop, would you?"

"Certainly not, Miss Wellesley-Clegg. I should rather rip off one of my own limbs and eat it. I have just had a narrow escape in the company of the Dowager Countess."

"There, Aylesworth. You see, no gentleman of discernment would want to do such a thing."

"Jilted," Aylesworth says with a shrug.

Miss Wellesley-Clegg addresses her maid. "Oh, look, Hen. A hackney. Hail it if you will. It has been a delightful afternoon, sirs."

I don't believe that for a moment, not with the masculine jostling for favors I have seen since my arrival—of course, it probably has been delightful for her, being the center of attention.

Hen, the maid, who emits a strange, musical droning sound that I think is some sort of hymn, offers to take my parcels to Terrant's house, and plucks Darrowby's from his hand with an air of friendly contempt. She ushers Miss Wellesley-Clegg into the hackney, gives us a curt nod as though she is the mistress and we the servants, and we watch as the carriage drives away.

"Whew," Aylesworth comments. "She's a virago, to be sure—the maid, Darrowby, not the incomparable Philomena. What now, gentlemen? Why, we're but a few doors from Jackson's. Do you fancy a bout, Linsley?"

Carrotte closes his notebook with a snap.

"Thank you, no, sir. I must escort the Dowager Countess home. Possibly Carrotte could oblige you."

Carrotte blushes deep red and drops his pencil.

I'm damned if I'll bend over anywhere in Aylesworth's vicinity and step back.

"Did I not just see the Dowager Countess in the company of Admiral Riley?" Aylesworth produces a quizzing glass and twirls it in his fingers.

"Possibly. She's kind enough to take an interest in him—he's not much used to society. He's the late earl's second cousin, but has been at sea these many years."

Aylesworth smirks in an unpleasant way and holds out his arm to Carrotte. "Well, sir, we must away. Your servant, Linsley, Darrowby."

Darrowby meanwhile stares in the direction the hackney has taken, bearing his beloved away. He looks so lovelorn and bereft I invite him to dine with me at a nearby chop-house, thinking that he must keep his strength up; besides, my mother is nowhere in sight, and I consider my filial duty done.

Miss Wellesley-Clegg

I am quite fond of Hen, who is a wonder with stains and ripped hems, and, in refreshing contrast to Mama, hardly speaks a word. However, she regards me with disapproval as the hackney bumps homeward, and I busy myself undoing one of my parcels, knowing she is about to pass judgment. Her soft drone about sin and retribution halts (she favors the sort of lurid hymn that my ancestress, Miss Hallelujah Clegg, probably sang).

"You're leading that nice young gentleman on," she pronounces and folds her arms.

"Indeed? I'm sure I do not know what you mean." I unroll a length of ribbon and lay it against my skirts for contrast. Yes, it will do.

"You know well enough, miss. That Mr. Darrowby." Her tone is one of kindly contempt.

"Oh. I thought you meant Lord Aylesworth." Of course I know whom she means, but I do not intend to involve myself in an argument with Hen.

"Him!" She snorts. "He's not interested in *you*, miss, and that poet fellow is no better."

"Oh! You think not? What have you heard?" Is Aylesworth, too, snapped up by a conniving widow? Has Carrotte found his muse?

She makes a huffing sound. The carriage jolts to a stop once again, and a small child appears at the window, rapping on the glass.

I let the window down, to Hen's silent disapproval.

A small boy, his hair matted, and dirt smudged on his face, grins at me. "Buy a gingerbread man, miss? Only a ha'penny. Three for a penny."

Maybe my sisters would enjoy them, and I'd like to sweeten up Hen before she complains to Mama about my alleged flirtation. I buy three and watch the boy dart off into the crowd as the carriage starts again.

"Probably made of sawdust and heaven knows what," Hen grumbles as she bites the head off her gingerbread man.

"Oh, that's strange." I examine the interior of the carriage. "Where did my ribbon go?"

Hen sighs. "Stolen by him, miss, I expect. You had it in your hand as you opened the window. They're a wicked lot, these Londoners. They'll all burn in hellfire, you mark my words." She brushes crumbs from her cloak with a righteous air.

"I didn't think it was that good a match. Besides, I'll have to go and look at that bonnet again. I'll try for a better color then."

Hen, her gingerbread man dismembered and devoured, resumes her singing. And then she takes me by surprise. "There's only one real man among the lot of them, miss, but his family wouldn't let him marry you. They're too proud, by all accounts, and he's no money of his own, and he's a wicked rake from all I hear."

"Whom do you mean, Hen?"

"Why, that Mr. Linsley." She grins. "And you'd best be careful of him, miss."

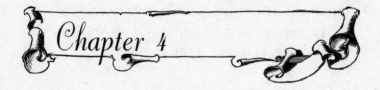

Chapter 4

Miss Philomena Wellesley-Clegg

List of available gentlemen as of this day:

1. ~~Lord Elmhurst.~~ Succumbed to the charms of
Lady Caroline Bludge.

2. ~~Lord Aylesworth.~~ Affections engaged elsewhere, according to Hen, who is so often right
in these matters.

3. ~~The Mad Poet~~. Ditto.

4. Viscount Elverton. Still my mama's favorite.

5. Tom Darrowby, whom I cannot avoid seeing as he is secretary to my brother-in-law Mr. Pullen and a great friend of the family.

6. Mr. Inigo Linsley.

Mr. Inigo Linsley? Heavens, he is by all accounts wicked and feckless, although Julia seems fond enough of him. I shall be wise and virtuous concerning Mr. Linsley. I may practice flirting with him, and I may even dance with him at the ball tonight, but I shall certainly not allow him to take liberties of any sort whatsoever, even if I think no one would find out. Absolutely not. Besides, it is as Hen says— his family, who are proud and haughty, would never allow even their youngest and most insignificant son to marry into Trade, and I am sure Mama and Papa would not allow me to form an alliance with a man of such bad reputation. Not that I should wish to do such a thing.

I do hope he will wear the dark blue satin coat and breeches tonight, but I resolve to think no more about the latter, which are pleasingly tight, and where, for some reason, I cannot help looking.

Lady Stelling's ball is the most dreadful crush, and my heart sinks as I see the jovial red face and hedgehog-like hair of Elverton bearing down like a French privateer. I had hoped, in the crowd, to be safe from precipitate proposals, so

I rush to the ladies' retiring room with my sister Diana, the Hon. Mrs. Pullen, and hide there until we consider it safe.

When we emerge like desperate brigands creeping down a cliff—I have been reading one of Mrs. Radcliffe's horrid novels on and off all this week—we take refuge with my aunt Rowbotham, who terrifies most, but whom I quite like. She folds me in a tender embrace, the ostrich feathers on her turban quivering almost as much as her chins, and Diana and I sneeze as snuff floats over us.

She introduces me to Ensign Something. I regret I never did discover his name, but he was apparently captured for the evening to hold Aunt Rowbotham's constant companion, her pug Roland.

Elverton approaches to ask me for a dance. To my great delight, Roland, who has been fed too many tidbits from the supper room, is sick on Elverton's feet. I am only too glad to escape with Ensign Something. I do wonder how the Battle of Trafalgar was won by our navy, for he can scarcely follow the steps of the dance. As usual, I have to explain that we are not *those* Wellesleys.

On the theory of doing my unpleasant duty as quickly as possible, I dance next with Elverton. He pays me the usual peculiar compliments, and I tell him that while he was away, washing his feet, I have been claimed for the rest of the evening. It is a dreadful lie, for I am only to dance with my brother-in-law Mr. Pullen.

Elverton then entertains me with stories about Sirius, the most affectionate, intelligent, loving, faithful hound in all England, for the entirety of the set. If I were not standing and moving, I should have fallen asleep. I entertain myself with thoughts of that certain bonnet, at whose shrine I did homage today, until I remind myself that I must not smile lest he see it as encouragement.

"'Pon my word, Miss Wellesley-Clegg, you remind me of my little Guernsey cow," Elverton says. Well, at least it is a change of subject from Sirius, the dog who should be Prime Minister and Cabinet together, if Elverton is to be believed.

"Why, thank you, sir." I must confess I am somewhat puzzled by the compliment, if that is indeed what he intends.

He leads me back towards Mama, gripping my arm as though he wishes to slip a halter over my head and milk me. Oh, dreadful thought. The horror!

Standing next to Mama is Mr. Tom Darrowby, who steps toward me, one hand held out, and his smile is so sweet and honest I immediately feel guilty. In his dark green coat and breeches he looks almost handsome, for the color shows off his chestnut-brown hair and dark eyes to great advantage. Oh, it is such a pity . . .

"Moo," says a voice behind me.

It is Mr. Inigo Linsley, and I am almost glad to see him.

"I believe we are engaged to dance, Miss Wellesley-Clegg, if you'll excuse us, Elverton."

"Oh, yes, indeed we are, to be sure." Goodness, I babble like a fool, and I drop my fan.

"Allow me, Miss Wellesley-Clegg."

Mr. Linsley stoops, so do I, and our skulls crack together, dislodging the silk flowers in my hair.

"Good God, my dear woman, do you seek to render me insensible?"

Dear woman! He called me his dear woman! I am speechless with delight.

He hands me my fan and a handful of silk flowers.

Oh, dear. There is a flower caught on his coat. Well, not really his coat. Lower down, in fact hardly his coat at all. It is in fact perilously close to the area at which I vowed I should look no more.

"Allow me, sir."

He jumps backwards, and makes a most peculiar grunting noise.

"Philly!"

"Yes, Mama."

Under pretence of repairing the damage done to my hair, she mutters, "One dance only and pray do not flirt with him for people stare enough already and we do not want to upset dear Elverton as I am convinced he will make an offer although, of course, he must speak to your dear papa but it would be so charming if passion propels him to address you first and we should be prepared to overlook any hint of impropriety under the circumstances and Philly my dear what about Darrowby he is most dreadfully in love with you and may yet ask first indeed we will be stuck between a rock and a hard place then to be sure but only in a good sort of way."

In my usual awe at Mama's ability to fire off so many words without drawing breath, I nod, hoping I reek of filial devotion. Papa, I know, could not care less. He currently agonizes over a letter from my brother Robert, reporting that the floor of the butler's pantry has caved in, taking with it half of the third-best china.

"Our dance is a waltz, Miss Wellesley-Clegg."

Heavens! "How delightful," I quaver foolishly.

He smiles. It is a charming smile; well, charming in a way that reveals a lot of large, white teeth, and reminds me of the revered Sirius. I am glad Inigo does not drool. The one time Elverton brought Sirius to call, he slobbered all over my gown—the dog, that is—then lay quiet at his master's feet. There, he gnawed his way through the leg of a Hepplewhite chair, much to Mama's annoyance.

"What are you thinking about?" He offers his arm.

"Why, that if you wore a lace cap and spectacles, you would make a passing good wolf."

"Indeed." His smile grows wide and thoughtful. "You should have to enter my bedchamber to witness that phenomenon."

I almost trip over my own feet as he leads me onto the floor. "So you are also in the habit of wearing old ladies' nightrails?"

"That is a vice I have no compulsion to acquire, Miss Wellesley-Clegg. Although you might wish to visit my bedchamber to make sure."

"I am sure I should wish to do no such thing." I attempt a haughty toss of the head at the moment his hand lands on my waist, and I fear the effect is one of a nervous wobble, as though I suffer from some distracting ailment.

"What a great pity." His other hand clasps mine. "For if you did, Miss Wellesley-Clegg, I should gobble you up straightaway."

Oh, heavens, these men. What is strange is that although Elverton's desire to milk me makes me want to rush shrieking from his presence, the idea of being gobbled up by Mr. Linsley has a peculiar sort of attraction. I do, in fact, feel quite warm in a way of which ladies rarely talk (except in ladies' cloakrooms, retiring-rooms, bedchambers of close female friends and sisters, walks in the park, viewing exhibits, waiting to be asked to dance at Almack's, et cetera).

"I see you are not indifferent to the idea of being devoured by me."

Oh, botheration. Apparently he reads my mind.

I concentrate on the steps and the music, not letting myself harbor delicious, wicked thoughts of Mr. Linsley in bed, baring his wolf-like teeth. I wonder if he wears a silly nightcap like Papa's? I do hope not. One-two-three. . . one-two-three . . . And a nightshirt? Or would he, possibly, be unclothed?

For the first time in my life I understand why the waltz is considered an indecent dance.

"So, are you engaged yet to that dolt?"

"I beg your pardon, sir?"

"Elverton, you silly little ninny. Or possibly Darrowby. They buzz around you like bees around a hive."

Heavens! First he calls me his dear woman, and now a silly little ninny, and compares me to a beehive, which no one has ever done before. I tread on his foot in my excitement.

"Why, no, Mr. Linsley, I am engaged to neither gentleman, and that is a most impertinent question."

He grins. How warm and large his hand is on my waist!

"Miss Wellesley-Clegg, you are quite delightful when you pretend to be offended."

"I *am* offended, sir." He thinks I am quite delightful! I get out of step and release a small shower of silk flowers.

"Dear me, you are quite disordered. Let us repair outside and make all well."

Before I know it, he has danced me through the open doors onto the balcony outside, where I am beyond the sight of my chaperones. There are a few other couples out here, standing close together, who pay us no attention whatsoever.

I am alone with a man of bad reputation. I cannot wait to tell my sister.

"Do you wish to scream and run to your mama?" We are no longer dancing, but he still has one hand on my waist.

"No, sir. You do not frighten me." Oh, but he does, but it is in a very good way.

He takes a step closer while pulling me towards him, and I am now pressed close to him. Some bits of me, despite my stays, squish up against him . . . and he is interesting. Bony and hard, and very, very warm, with a faint scent of lavender. He is not so tall as that great gangly Elverton, so he has only to bend his head a little to . . .

"I believe I am about to kiss you, Miss Wellesley-Clegg."

"Oof." My breath is entirely gone for some reason.

His lips brush mine. They are very soft and gentle, and I remember their contours as I have observed them from time to time—the full lower lip that now twitches, although I think that is the wrong word, against mine. It is both shocking and innocent. I open my mouth to ask him if that is all that is involved, for why should people make such a fuss if that is all there is? And then his mouth brushes mine again, with the tip of his tongue, warm and soft and wet, reaching to touch mine.

Did he really mean to do that? He tastes delicious. Of wine, naturally, and, although this sounds most silly, of velvet, and music, and the smoothness of a seashell. And beneath all, he is the wild creature who will eat me up.

Now I want to eat him too.

Mr. Inigo Linsley

Devil take it.

A fellow does not want to open his eyes to see his dear mama and his eldest brother at the foot of his bed.

It reminds me of my ill-fated army career, the shortest in history, a full twenty-two hours, which ended in an ignominious fall from a balcony and a broken leg. The colonel told me my conduct was unbecoming to the uniform. How could it have been? I was naked as Adam, my regimentals strewn on the colonel's bedchamber floor where his lady had ripped them off me but fifteen ecstatic minutes before.

And only to think that had the colonel not come home early that night, I could have been gloriously blown to pieces for king and country on the field of Waterloo. And then, instead of being known as the wastrel son of the family, I would have been elevated to damned near sainthood.

That time I woke with a demon in my leg, another in my head, and a damned parson mumbling of fornicators and adulterers, for I was not expected to live.

As then, my immediate thought is: *What the devil have I done this time?*

Terrant has his older-brother sanctimonious smirk pasted onto his face, the look of a man doing his duty at the expense of his debauched younger brother and making sure everyone knows how much he enjoys it.

"Why, Mama and Pudgebum," I say, using the nickname he had at school, something I know will annoy him. "Good morning."

My head and heart pound. Foxed, yes, I was certainly foxed. It's expected of a gentleman. But not overly so.

"You must marry, Inigo," Mama pronounces.

Oh, dear God. "Wh—who?" I quaver.

She frowns. "*Whom*, Inigo."

"This is the way of it, Ratsarse," my brother says, using my own hated childhood nickname. "You need someone to bring you up to snuff."

"I do?"

"So," Terrant continues, "the family has decided—regretfully you slept through the meeting, which concluded half an hour ago—that you should marry. As soon as your engagement is certain, you shall have Weaselcopse Manor and its estate as your own, and to which you shall bring your bride."

Since I already act as land agent for Weaselcopse Manor, and a handful of other smaller estates the family owns, I am only thankful I am to inherit some land in good order. "Why, brother, how exceedingly generous of you."

"I should expect you to continue in your duties elsewhere." Terrant may lose income from Weaselcopse but he's too tightfisted to pay someone else.

"Shall I not be too busy dandling my children on my knee?"

"Which brings us to another matter," Mama says. The dear woman has an unpleasant grin on her face. I anticipate she is to have revenge for the years of worry her troublesome youngest son has caused. She nods at Pudgebum.

"You may come in, now, sir!"

A black-clad, obsequious figure bows his way into the room at my brother's command.

"We wish to make sure," my sweet, retiring mama says, "that everything is in working order. This is Dr. Ferguson."

"I beg your pardon, Mama?" I clutch the sheets to myself. Everything in working order? Surely she cannot mean . . . no, it is obscene.

"You lead a life of dissolution, yet have shown no inclination to marry. What do you expect us to think?"

"I may be dissolute, but I am no fool! I have spent a considerable sum on—"

Pudgebum glowers at me, shaking his head, to remind me that our dear mama is a creature of delicate sensibilities whose mind may not be sullied by the mention of sheep gut, except possibly in the context of sausages.

Dr. Ferguson ingratiates himself forward and drops a leather case, which lands with an ominous rattle, on my bed. His nose is long, embellished with an unhealthy drip. He produces a small porcelain vessel and shoves it at me, spluttering something in a barbarous, onion-scented Scottish accent.

Mama leaves the room in a rustle of self-righteousness.

"Piss," my brother translates.

"Piss on you," I say, with the wit and grace for which I am renowned, and resign myself to my fate.

This must be divine punishment for kissing that pretty, silly, affected husband-hunting butterfly, Miss Wellesley-Clegg. I shall never do it again.

Never.

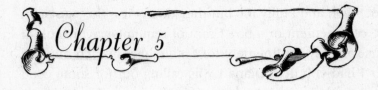

Chapter 5

Miss Philomena Wellesley-Clegg

D——n.

If I were a man, of course, I should have the privilege of spelling out the word. It seems my sister, as right as rain and stuffing herself like a pig in the supper room last night, has good reason for her hearty appetite, thus ruining my bonnet and gossip plans.

"I shall die," she moans from her sofa. Her face is much the same color as her morning gown, a misty green that otherwise would be quite attractive. "I shall never get in whelp again. Oh, if only Pullen were not so passionate a man."

Pullen, passionate? I wonder he has time to take his nose from his collection of butterflies, which I have always considered the true love of his life.

"Now my dear I was like this every morning all the while I carried you and Philly too but they do say it is the sign of an easy confinement or a boy I cannot remember which oh of course an easy confinement for I remember not ten minutes after I had you dear Diana I was calling out for some good roast beef do you think we should call your maid my dear?"

"No. Pray do not talk of food, Mama." She waves away her angelic son James, who toddles around the room with a toy clutched to his chest. "Show your horse to your aunt."

"No," he says in a singsong voice. "No, no, no." He lurches against my knee, stuffs a finger into his nose, removes it and smears my gown. I am thankful it is the unfortunate yellow muslin, from which the ink removal has not been altogether successful.

"Sit on Aunt Philly's lap like a good boy," my sister says in a faint voice.

I brace myself, remembering what happened last time James sat on my lap, and arrange the inkblot strategically under his inadequately padded bottom. He climbs up, with the help of very sharp elbows and knees, and stares at me.

"No," he says as an opening conversational gambit.

I stick my tongue out at him.

He returns the courtesy.

"Pray do not encourage him Philly well my dear we have high hopes of Elverton . . ." Mama launches into a frenzied monologue of how soon Elverton will propose, in much the same way gentlemen will talk of a favorite in a horse race.

Had Diana been in good health, she would have reminded Mama of my comparative youth—but heavens, at almost twenty I am perilously close to being an old maid—and the possibility of bigger fish in the matrimonial sea. As it is, she groans occasionally, a sound Mama takes as encouragement, while I make faces at my sister across the room.

James makes faces at her too.

". . . and James my dear if you should pull such a face and the wind turns in the other direction for sure you shall be stuck like that forever and all will say what a shame it is that such a pretty boy has turned so plain . . ."

"It is not true," I whisper to my nephew. "She told me that, and I tested it."

"No, no, no," he responds.

It is about as rewarding as a conversation with Elverton, whose only saving grace in comparison is that he does not stick his finger up his nose in my presence. As my sister groans on the sofa, my mother prattles, and James alternates between holding his breath and repeating his favorite word, Tom Darrowby enters the room and bows.

"Mr. Pullen sends his regards, madam," he says to my mother, "and wishes to know if you would still like to borrow the music for the younger Misses Wellesley-Clegg."

"Oh the music yes indeed Tom it is so kind of you to remember for my dear children are so avid for new pieces to play they are the most prodigiously talented girls and Philly will be only too happy to help you choose the pieces why Philly my dear do you have something in your eye that you wink so hard at me you may go with Mr. Darrowby why it is hardly improper since our families are such great friends her modesty is charming is it not Tom . . ."

I am swept along by her words as if in a flooded torrent, and somehow find myself being escorted by Tom toward the library, and I must confess I am quite put out.

"So, how are you, Philly? I hardly have the chance to have a word with you these days." He gazes at me with his soft brown eyes. "Is it still all right for me to address you by your first name? You have not become a grand London miss, I hope."

Of course I have to say it is no matter. After all, I have addressed him in public as Tom, something I see now is most irregular, particularly with Aylesworth, the worst gossip in London, present. I have always called him Tom, and it is a hard habit to break.

"I was hoping," he continued, "that we should have a dance together last night, but you were so much in demand. I barely saw you after you danced with Linsley."

"Oh, indeed yes, it was a capital ball." I add, hoping it will make him feel better, "But you and I have danced together a hundred times already, Tom, in the country, and I expect we shall dance together a hundred times more."

"I should like to think we could share a lot more than that, Philly." He opens the library door and ushers me inside. "I must admit I am concerned about you. I should not like you to fall into the clutches of an adventurer."

"Oh, I am too sensible for that." At least, I hope I am. I think again of Mr. Linsley's threat to gobble me up and go all shivery inside as though I am catching a chill.

"Well, I suppose it is natural you should enjoy London.

Young ladies do like that sort of thing." He lifts a large leather folder of music from a shelf and spreads it out on the table. "As for me, I miss home, and the easy, neighborly society we enjoyed there."

I make a noncommittal noise, remembering long evenings at cards while my mother talked and Tom's mother threw in the occasional odd comment about the health of Darrowby family members none of us had met. I open the folder and turn the pages, picking out pieces I hope my sisters will enjoy. The sheets of music smell musty and my nose itches.

"And I think after you have had your fill of the season, Philly, and Parliament is in recess for the summer, we shall all return to Lancashire and then maybe—"

I interrupt his proposal—for I am sure that is what he intends—with a loud sneeze.

"I beg your pardon," I gasp in relief. "Oh, this is splendid. Lydia and Charlotte will be most grateful."

"Philly, they play piano. Why are you taking them a piece for two violins and the violoncello?"

"Oh." I give a nervous giggle. "My mistake. Thank you, Tom."

"And the duet for baritone and soprano? Does Mr. Wellesley-Clegg sing?"

"Not really." Oh, I am making a complete fool of myself. And then my mind is made up. I am from Lancashire, where we pride ourselves on plain speech. "Tom, please do not ask me to marry you."

He bites his lip and looks quite hurt. "Philly, will you tell me there is no one else? May I hope?"

When I do not reply, he mutters, "Elverton, I suppose."

I do not like to tell him that my current list of eligible gentlemen is down to the last three, all of whom, for various reasons, are entirely unsuitable.

I grab a handful of what I hope are piano duets. "Tom, I should like us to be friends, for that is what we have always been."

"Friends are honest with each other."

I stuff the music under one arm and try to think of an appropriate response. Part of me—the rational, sensible Philomena who does not waltz with disreputable men and allow herself to be kissed by them, although to be sure it was only once, and it will never happen again—urges me to encourage him. We know each other so well, after all. It would be a good, appropriate match, and my fortune would surely aid his parliamentary career (for such are his aspirations).

But the other part of me, the wanton who has not been able to stop thinking of Mr. Linsley's voice and touch, and his mouth, particularly his mouth (and that business of the tongue, which bothers me far more than it should)—that part of me wants to rage at Tom for his presumption.

"I think I should go back to Mama now," I say, as we face each other like a pair of hares about to box each other. It is a particularly feeble excuse—I did not bleat about my mama when Mr. Linsley (the vile seducer) lured me onto the terrace—and I am ashamed to behave like a milk-and-water miss.

He makes a gesture that is half nod, half bow, and opens the library door for me.

I sweep past him, leaving, I am sure, a smell of musty old paper in my wake.

I am absolutely sure that we are not friends now, and I am not happy about it. I do not like to treat Tom so, even if he has done his share of unpleasant things to me, although some time ago, it is true, and usually involving spiders, worms, and one time, an unexpected immersion in a pond.

What is worse, I cannot stop thinking about Mr. Linsley's kiss, or, as I should probably refer to it, The Kiss. How can a few seconds, a touch of lips, make the world seem an entirely new and wondrous place? How can anything so wicked be so comforting and sweet at the same time? And the tongue, too. I should like to ask Diana whether that is customary, but I fear a mention of anything entering anyone's mouth might make her puke, and thus sully my memory.

I should also like to ask her whether it is the done thing for the gentleman to say, "Well, that is enough of that," and dance the lady back into the ballroom to join the others.

Maybe he was embarrassed by the tongue episode, too. Or he was alarmed, as I was, by the sinuous writhing of the lady and gentleman not six feet from us. I wonder who it was, for her face was quite hidden against his. She wore a very pretty headdress, comprising some plumes and sparkly things, surely not real jewels, they must have been paste, and loops of a very elegant braided cord. But I digress.

How can I look Mr. Linsley in the face, knowing his tongue, accidentally or otherwise, has touched mine? I should like to do it again, so long as there is no chance I should be ruined and packed off to our disintegrating Lancashire house. Were it any other gentleman, I should of course consult Julia, but she is his sister-in-law! It is impossible.

Thank heaven I have the pressing subject of bonnets to distract me, and so later that day I set out with Hen to Bond Street to pay tribute to the delightful confection of the milliner's art that has haunted my thoughts. And this time, it is perfect. I do not have any gentlemen hovering around, paying me ridiculous compliments, and generally getting in the way. Aylesworth, I am afraid, spent far too much time whispering *sotto voce* comments to The Mad Poet that I could not fully catch.

"What do you think of this, Hen?" In delaying the delicious moment of sartorial consummation I try on a lesser masterpiece.

"*. . . cast into that everlasting pit . . .* Not your color, Miss Philomena."

I pick up the bonnet that was my first love, a paragon of simplicity, elegance, and delicate quilling. I am not so sure of the ruching of the ribbon on the brim, now I examine it more closely, and it really is a rather peculiar shape. Eyes shut, I place it on my head, tying a fetching bow beneath my left ear. When I open my eyes to admire it, I feel only a sinking sensation in my stomach.

What I see is only a bonnet.

Fashionable, flattering, and highly expensive, but still only a bonnet.

Only a bonnet? I, Philomena Wellesley-Clegg, the *arbiteuse* of headwear, thinks this item of beauty is *only a bonnet*?

"Very pretty, miss . . . *and the blood of the lamb . . .*"

"I shall buy it." I remove the offending—no, to be quite fair, the *inoffensive* item—and let Hen make arrangements with the shopkeeper. Papa will have a fit when the bill comes, unless a piece of our Lancashire house collapses to distract him.

Oh dear. I did not realize that the changed world brought about by The Kiss included the toppling of the one great pleasure in my life from its pedestal.

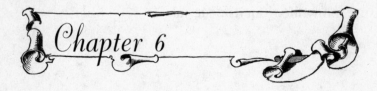

Chapter 6

Mr. Inigo Linsley

As my sister-in-law says, I have no idea how to deal with women of quality. All of the ladies who are considered diamonds of the first water amongst this season's debutantes, all possessed of fortune, represent only feminine bundles of flaws to me.

List of possible wives

1. ~~Lady Caroline Bludge~~. Thank God.

2. Miss Anne Dyson. Laughs like a wild beast, one inch taller than I. Dreadful mama.

3. Lady Susan Ponsonby. Incapable of conversation, smiles too much. Disabused me of the notion a woman's bosom could never be too large the last, and only time, I waltzed with her. Dreadful mama.

4. Miss Evelyn Bottomley. Unfortunately but appropriately named, see bosom, above. Insane papa. Dreadful mama.

5. Miss Celia Blundell. Eats all the time, would bring estate to ruin as she chomps through standing crops. Dreadful mama.

6. Lady Amelia Hartwell. Perpetual giggler given to excessively bad performances on the pianoforte, as on the last, memorable occasion when that silly Miss Wellesley-Clegg almost caught me *in flagrante* with Caroline. Dreadful mama.

7. Miss Barbara Winsdell. Much given to sighing over poetry, casting eyes heavenward, and indulging in serious discussions. Smelly pet dog. Dreadful mama.

8. Miss Philomena Wellesley-Clegg.

Miss Wellesley-Clegg? Has my lust for Weaselcopse Manor knocked all sense out of my head? For one thing, she is Trade. My family would make life extremely unpleasant if I dared propose to her. True, she was extremely pleasant to kiss, and she displayed an amusing blend of wantoness and innocence, but . . . *Miss Wellesley-Clegg?*

Trade. She is Trade. The noble blood of the Linsleys cannot mingle with that of commoners. Never. They own a *coal mine*—the horror!

On the one hand, the others are not particularly likable women. In fact, the only resemblance to them is that Miss Wellesley-Clegg is also saddled with a particularly dreadful mama.

Sweet, funny, pliable, lovely Miss Wellesley-Clegg.

Damnation.

I go in search of my sister-in-law, and try first the drawing-room. The door is closed, and as I open it, I hear a scuffle, and come face-to-face with my mother, who looks particularly enraged.

The Admiral, who is becoming as much a part of the household as our furniture, stands at the mantelpiece, somewhat red in the face and adusting his neckcloth.

"What the devil do you want?" my mother snaps.

"I beg your pardon, madam." I back out of the room, giving the Admiral a curt nod, and run Julia to earth in the morning room, busy with her household accounts.

"What are you doing with a Bible, Inigo?"

"I must have you swear on it, my dear Julia."

She lays down her pen and frowns at me. She is always very proper, though from hints Pudgebum has dropped, not always so while performing certain marital duties. And I was quite shocked to find evidence of activities outside the bedchamber—Julia's busk lying on the floor in a room with no lock.

"I am surprised a thunderbolt has not felled you, you infidel. What am I supposed to swear?"

"To silence. It is nothing improper, just that a gentleman of my acquaintance has an interest in a lady of yours, and naturally it would be most embarrassing if word got out to either of them." I peer over her shoulder. "Your last column adds up to fifty-seven, which is four shillings and nine pence."

"Oh dear me, yes. Thank you. I swear not a word shall pass my lips, and you know, Inigo, I have never seen you blush before."

The minx.

I finger my neckcloth, which has become suddenly tight. "It is rather warm in here."

"Oh, nonsense. I suppose it is Philomena."

I give up all attempts at subtlety. "How did you guess?"

"Well, I am neither blind nor deaf. Inigo, she is a sweet girl and my dearest friend, and you shall not break her heart." She looks at me with all seriousness now.

"I have no intention of doing anything of the sort!"

"Or dishonor her."

"Good God, Julia, have you no shame?"

"I do, but you do not, sir." She thrusts the Bible at me. "Swear it, Inigo. Swear you will only offer her marriage."

"Well, obviously I cannot do that. The family is in Trade. Our mother would never approve. Incidentally, why is that Admiral always in our house?"

"Sev?" She dips her pen into her inkwell. "The Dowager Countess is fond of him. He was a great friend of the late earl's when they were boys, and I think she enjoys talking to him. He is good company, Inigo, you must admit it. She misses your papa, you know."

"So do I."

"Terrant, too. I think he finds it hard, being the head of the family."

"Terrant isn't the head of the family. My mother is."

"So you may like to think, since you and Terrant and the rest of you are such milksops, under the thumb of—oh, Mama-in-law, what a pleasant surprise. How well that color suits you."

Mama ignores Julia and beckons to me. "Inigo, you shall accompany me on my morning calls."

"Yes, madam."

"Remember what I said," Julia whispers to me. "And remember, Inigo, she's as good as engaged to Tom Darrowby—the families have been friends for years, and although it is not a brilliant match, I believe they would be very happy together. And he's such a kind man. Please do not flirt with her."

I follow my mother out of the room.

Miss Wellesley-Clegg. Trade. Sweet, funny, lovely, pliable Miss Wellesley-Clegg. I believe her eyes are some sort of hazel. They change with the light and with her mood. Her hair is brown that picks up red and gold by candlelight. How can she be both so innocent and so fearless? She unsettles me mightily. This will not do. Dreadful mama. Trade. Dreadful mama.

I must remember her dreadful mama, for I cannot forget that kiss.

And I swore to nothing.

"I suppose we should call on those Wellesley-Cleggs, since you were condescending enough to dance with their chit last night," my dear mother remarks after an hour or so of vicious drawing-room banter. She has made several unfortunate hostesses writhe in shame and stifled fury, and now, like a prizefighter who has warmed up with a few lesser opponents, she wishes to take on someone worthy of her mettle.

I grunt in acquiescence.

"Trade, my dear," she reminds me, metaphorically flexing her knuckles.

Our arrival at the Wellesley-Cleggs' house interrupts an artistic endeavor in the foyer. Miss Wellesley-Clegg, swathed in a linen apron, and with her hair in wild curls around her face, is doing something to the statue on the plinth at the base of the staircase.

She steps off her chair to curtsey to us both.

My mother nods in acknowledgement, and sweeps into the drawing room to pick her corner.

I wait until the footman has closed the door behind her. "What are you about, Miss Wellesley-Clegg?"

"Oh, this . . ." She waves a hand at her work and steps up onto the chair again. "It is new, you see. Papa ordered it, and then Mama decided, that, well . . ." She blushes most becomingly.

"Ah. It is meant to be Hebe, cupbearer to the gods?"

"Mama thinks it is too unclothed."

"But that is how Hebe is traditionally represented, with one, ah, one . . . in that way." I stare at the offending bared breast, which is quite pretty. I wonder what . . .

"So I am attempting to paint her some more drapery." Her voice interrupts my musing on her own anatomy.

"On bronze, Miss Wellesley-Clegg? I don't think it's possible."

"Oh, but it is not bronze, Mr. Linsley. It is plaster, and I have scraped her to provide a surface for the paint, which is some left over from when we had the dining-room painted. It is a very fashionable color, and they just finished yesterday."

"Most handsome." So the imitation bronze Hebe is about to be decently covered with sky-blue draperies.

"Well, I hope it will be." She gazes at the statue, dips her paintbrush into a small bucket placed on the stairs, and hesitates. "There is only one problem. Her . . . well, I do not think it will convince anyone, because her . . ."

Oh say it, Miss Wellesley-Clegg. Say that word. I will her lips to part for the N.

". . . Because of the contours of the torso."

Damnation.

"Very true." Her own bosom is level with my head. What would she do if I pushed my face into . . . Enough. "May I suggest, Miss Wellesley-Clegg, that you, ah, remove the offending, ah, protrusion."

"An excellent idea, Mr. Linsley, and I had intended to do so." She removes a small sanding-block from the pocket of her apron. "But I was afraid I should crack the plaster, or remove too much."

"Allow me, Miss Wellesley-Clegg." I, after all, have considerable skill at handling the female anatomy.

She places her hand in mine to step from her chair. I have removed my gloves, of course, and her hand is bare and warm in mine.

She gives me a nervous half-smile.

"If you do not object, Miss Wellesley-Clegg, I believe I should remove my outer garment."

"Your . . . ?" Her eyes widen.

"My coat, that is."

"Oh, of course, Mr. Linsley."

Coat off, I mount the chair in my turn, thus finding myself eye-to-eye with Hebe, and begin the removal of her nipple. It is harder work than I expected, and I place a foot on the plinth to steady myself.

"Mr. Linsley, do be careful!"

At that point, there is a knock on the front door, the footman opens it, and I turn my head to see that fool Elverton, accompanied by a large dog, entering the house. Elverton looks somewhat surprised to see me, apparently embracing a statue in my shirtsleeves, one hand working on its bared breast.

"How d'ye do, Elverton," I say with as much carelessness as I can muster, caught in an unnatural act with a plaster goddess.

His damned dog advances and sniffs at the plinth in the way male dogs will do.

"Away, sir!" I bellow to the cur as one hind leg rises, and I reach down to swat at it with the sanding-block.

Too late, I realize the statue is not firmly affixed to the

plinth, and Hebe, I, and the bucket crash to the floor in a spray of plaster and blue paint. Miss Wellesley-Clegg shrieks, and the door to the drawing room flies open, revealing our respective mamas and a gaggle of other ladies.

"Now sir I hope you are not badly hurt lord that is too bad blue paint all over and poor Wellesley-Clegg's new statue in pieces Elverton you must think you are come into a madhouse I declare Philly that gown is now ruined such a shame for I think yellow suits you well do not you Elverton . . ."

"Good afternoon, Mrs. Wellesley-Clegg, ladies." To his credit, Elverton cuts her off in midflow with considerable adroitness. "If I may be so bold, I'm here to see Mr. Wellesley-Clegg."

An expectant hush falls over the assembled company. We all know what that means.

Beside me, someone gives a small gasp.

The silence is broken by a rhythmic scraping sound, and I turn my head, from my sprawled position on the floor, to observe the damned dog straddling the miraculously preserved left leg of Hebe.

"Call off your dog, Elverton!" I swipe at the idiot creature.

"What, pray, is in your hand, Inigo?"

Oh, Lord. My own dear mother. "A breast, madam. A plaster one."

She snorts, turns around, and marches back into the drawing-room.

Babbling continuously, Mrs. Wellesley-Clegg gives Elverton and the dog into the care of a footman, instructs another to see to cleaning the floor, and picks one of Hebe's fingers from her daughter's hair. Finishing with a comment about soap and water, and the availability of Mr. Wellesley-Clegg's valet, she leaves to attend her guests. The sound of her voice fades away as the drawing-room door closes again.

"Oh, bloody damnation!" Miss Wellesley-Clegg says.

Then she bursts into tears.

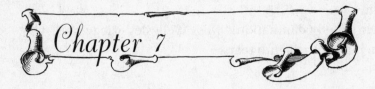

Chapter 7

Miss Philomena Wellesley-Clegg

I am mortified.

Everyone knows there is nothing a gentleman hates so much as the sight of a female in tears, but I cannot help it. Worse still, my tears are not of the sensitive, refined variety, but huge gulping sobs, accompanied by copious streaming from my nose.

I bury my face in my apron, even though I know blue paint will now be smeared onto my face, and hope that Mr. Linsley will retire to wash as Mama suggested.

And to think I almost said "nipple" in front of him! And he heard me swear most horribly!

"Miss Wellesley-Clegg, pray do not distress yourself." His voice is low and gentle. Oh, why does he have to be so kind? "Please, take my handkerchief."

His handkerchief is much the cleanest thing in the foyer, even with a large blue thumb-print on it. I blow my nose, revealing yet another unattractive feature—that when I do this, it is no delicate sniffle but the sound of an angry goose.

"I am dreadfully sorry about the statue." He prods a piece of it with his foot. "I shall replace it, of course. If possible, I shall find one of Hebe wearing a pelisse, requiring no further alteration."

"It is not that." I honk again into his handkerchief. "It is—it is that Elverton is requesting my hand, and of course Papa will say yes, and then I shall have to accept him, and I don't want to."

"Then don't."

"But there is no good reason to refuse him. Everyone looks down on us because we are in Trade, and I have two sisters in the schoolroom still, and I must marry as well, if not better, than my sister Diana."

"Oh, fustian, Miss Wellesley-Clegg. Tell Elverton and his hound to go to the devil." He looks quite annoyed, beneath the blue paint.

"You are in a shocking state, Mr. Linsley."

He nods. "You too." He puts his hand under my elbow and leads me out of the way of our servants, who have arrived with cloths, buckets, brooms, and other such stuff, to clean the wreckage of the foyer. The pungent odor of linseed oil rises in the air.

He sniffs, and sighs. "Do you care for cricket, Miss Wellesley-Clegg?"

"No." What does that have to do with anything? How typical of a man.

"Ah, well, you are not alone in your sex in having an indifference to the game. The odor of linseed oil reminded me, that is all." He takes the handkerchief from me, finds a dry corner, and wipes my face. "So you are determined to accept Elverton?"

"I can see no alternative. I must marry soon, and I must marry well."

"But you don't even like the fellow. Or his dog."

"Oh, pray, Mr. Linsley, if you wish to meddle in my affairs, run into the street and select a suitable bridegroom for me. I am sure there is a coachman or chimney-sweep who would suffice."

"I think we can do better than that."

"What do you mean?" A horrid, dreadful, breathless suspicion rises in my mind.

"Miss Wellesley-Clegg, at any moment Elverton's interview will be concluded and your fate will be sealed. And . . ."

The drawing-room door rattles, and he pulls open the nearest door, unfortunately the one to the water-closet beneath the stairs, where we take shelter as Mama's guests depart. All of them, except his mother, whose barks punctuate the limpid flow of Mama's never-ending conversation, have now gone.

Heavens, I am in a water-closet with a man of dubious reputation and I cannot even savor the moment. It is too bad. Already I feel the bonds of matrimony with Elverton close around my soul like iron.

Mr. Linsley inspects the apparatus with great interest. "The latest model, I see."

"Indeed, yes," I respond, trying for a similar, detached tone. "It is guaranteed odorless."

"And to think I blamed the dog. Well, Miss Wellesley-Clegg, pray do not stand on ceremony. Shall we sit?" He gestures to the double seat.

"Certainly not!"

"Very well." He leans toward me. "The problem I see is this. You are not averse to the idea of matrimony itself, just with Elverton. What you need, Miss Wellesley-Clegg, is a dispensable fiancé—one whom you can cast off whenever you choose. You need to know that your jilted gentleman will not expire of a broken heart, or challenge your new swain to a duel, or some such nonsense. Miss Wellesley-Clegg, I am your man. I regret there is not room enough for me to kneel."

"But—"

"And naturally, the engagement shall be secret until the end of the season, although I assure you, you shall discard me long before then, as enchanting a creature as you are."

"But why—"

"Say yes, madam. Do not deny me."

Goodness! His eyes burn in the dim light. He raises my hand to his mouth and we exchange blue paint in a sizzling, exciting sort of way.

"But why, Mr. Linsley? Why do *you* wish to do this?"

We hear masculine voices and footsteps as Elverton and Papa, their business concluded, walk past the water-closet and continue to the drawing room.

"I'll tell you later, you ninny. I have good reason, I assure you."

The drawing-room door opens.

"Well?" He is pressed up closer to me than he needs to be, even with the dimensions of the water-closet. My legs turn to jelly.

"Yes. Yes, I—"

"Capital!"

He drags me from the closet and positions us in the hall-way opposite the open door of the drawing-room, where even now, Mama, in full verbal flood, clasps Elverton's hands.

And Mr. Linsley kisses me.

I have been a fool. The Kiss was a tiny pale imitation of what he does now.

This is a real kiss, thrumming through me, humming in my belly, and on my back where his hand presses me to him as though we endeavor to keep a sheet of delicate pa-per between ourselves. His mouth closes over mine, and his tongue, dear Lord, his tongue is supple and wet, uncurling against mine. Right inside my mouth! His lips nibble and slide and press as his tongue partners mine in a far more wicked dance than any waltz. My legs quiver against his.

I can't breathe. I shall swoon. No, I will not. This is too wonderful to waste on a show of maidenly modesty and I must not miss a second. Oh, the feel of his hair under my hand, and his body, all hard and sinewy and so alive against mine, all that implied strength as though at any moment he might sweep me into his arms and carry me off to—

"Inigo!"

"Philomena!"

The cries of our respective mamas, and Sirius nosing between us in the vicinity of Mr. Linsley's breeches, inter-rupt us.

"Damn you, Linsley, Miss Wellesley-Clegg is engaged to me!" Everton pushes towards us, his face red and furious.

"I am not, sir. You have not asked me." My voice is quite breathless, as though I have run up the stairs, and my face feels wet around my mouth and hot elsewhere.

"And neither has this scoundrel, I'll be bound." Elverton clenches a fist.

"Oh, yes, he did. And I have accepted."

Mr. Linsley clasps his hand in mine and shoves Sirius away with one foot. "Passion overtook us in the water-closet, where Miss Wellesley-Clegg agreed to make me the happiest of men, Elverton."

The Dowager Countess falls onto the sofa, her heels drumming on the floor, and offers a series of short screams like a screech owl in voice.

"Out for the count, by God," Mr. Linsley murmurs, rather unkindly, I think.

Mama, shocked into silence for maybe ten seconds, bursts her banks. "Why Philly what would your papa say oh he is here oh my dear what shall we do with this girl pray someone fetch my vinaigrette and tea no we must have brandy it is a dreadful shock to me too but fortunately I can bear it for I am made of sterner stuff but oh Philly he is all covered in blue paint and only a younger son and a rake and a wastrel from all I hear and has no fortune to speak of oh my dear Mr. Wellesley-Clegg we are undone that our daughter should marry such a man what are we to do and to think she turned down Elverton after encouraging him so shockingly why everyone talked of it where is the brandy and now I shall not be able to hold up my head in society—"

"That's enough, Mrs. Wellesley-Clegg." Papa has spoken.

The ensuing silence is broken by the sound of Sirius's rhythmic lapping in the water-closet.

Mama sinks onto the sofa next to the Dowager Countess and raises a handkerchief to her face.

Servants arrive with fresh tea and brandy, and Hen appears with a vinaigrette. It is quite the most exciting thing to have happened in our house in weeks, and poor Diana will be sad to have missed it. My hand is still in Mr. Linsley's, and he gives me a hint of one of his wicked, sideways smiles, where his lips turn up just a little, and my legs quiver.

Hen stops by me on her way out. "You've made a right upset, miss, for all he's a handsome gentleman."

Mr. Linsley winks at her, and she departs upstairs, a ditty about saints casting down their crowns into a glassy sea in her wake. I wonder why they should do such a thing unless they plan to dive in after them for entertainment, and I must say it seems a strange way to spend eternity.

"Come on in, Philly, Mr. Linsley. We'd best talk," Papa says, hands beneath his coattails.

"Indeed, sir, we should, for I've never been so insulted in my life!" Elverton glares at me. "The lady gave me every encouragement, sir. Why, her own mother says as much. She is nothing but a shameless flirt."

"I am not!"

"You should leave, sir." Mr. Linsley does not change his posture, but his voice is very, very cool, and Elverton steps back from him.

"Don't forget Sirius," I offer helpfully.

We advance into the drawing-room, Elverton leaves, and we hear the front door close after him.

A dust sheet has been thrown over the smaller sofa, and Papa indicates I should sit there. Mr. Linsley gives my hand a final squeeze and releases me. How handsome he looks even when splattered in blue paint from head to toe!

"Well, now, Mr. Linsley," my papa says, "what do you know of subsidence?"

Chapter 8

Mr. Inigo Linsley

"Very little, sir. Subsidence was not a subject much in demand at Winchester. But I do know a great deal about field drains."

"Field drains, eh? Good, good."

Dear heavens, this family confounds me. First, this dry stick of a papa, a short, mild man who peers at me over his spectacles with an unnerving shrewdness. He reminds me of my tailor and bootmaker, masters at hinting that I am in their debt while leading me on to commit greater foolishness. He does not seem even particularly concerned—at least, not at this moment—that I have been caught red-handed dishonoring his daughter, and am responsible for the violation and destruction of his piece of statuary.

Mrs. Wellesley-Clegg has missed a calling as an otter, for never have I met a person who lasts so long without drawing breath. Yet she has a particular streak of common sense under her babbling exterior, and I suspect it would be unwise to underestimate her.

As for the adorable Philomena, she is the most mysterious of all, and I cannot define what it is about her that intrigues me so. She is quite short—and as I am not the tallest of men, this is an advantage—and she fits in my arms perfectly. She takes to kissing like a duck to water (to be sure, this is an aquatic family) and I find myself staring at her pretty mouth, a perfect Cupid's bow, now reddened and puffy from my rapaciousness. As for the rest, her eyes are rather round, but it suits her, her nose slightly snub with an unfashionable scattering of freckles, and there is a charming hollow with a blue vein above her collarbone that I long to kiss.

Her papa clears his throat in a significant sort of way to gain my wandering attention. "This is an odd sort of courtship, Mr. Linsley. Why, when I wooed Mrs. Wellesley-Clegg, or, as she was then, Miss Maria Cutting—"

"Maria? Maria Cutting?" My mother jolts upright on the sofa. "Not Maria Cutting who was at Miss Grimsley's Academy for Gentlewomen?"

"No it cannot be why I declare it is so Betsy Wormworth of all people oh my dear you know I have always thought you looked familiar and could not fathom why it has been an age and to think we should meet again . . ." The trades-man's wife and the Dowager Countess fall into each other's arms. I am even more dumbfounded that my mama actu-ally allowed anyone to address her as Betsy.

Mr. Wellesley-Clegg pours me a glass of brandy, refills his own, and passes the decanter to the two reunited school-girls, who now sob on each other's shoulders.

"Aye, well, you see Mr. Linsley," he continues. "I need to make sure you're a fit husband for my little Philly. I don't put a great deal of stock in titles and families and such. You'd best tell me why I should give her away to you. I'm not a great believer in fits of passion either. They don't last, you see."

"Papa!" his daughter cries.

"Philly, my dear, this is between us at the moment. If I'm not satisfied, Mr. Linsley can leave this house a free man, and no harm done. I'd high hopes for Elverton, you know, a fine, upstanding gentleman."

Miss Wellesley-Clegg takes a quick swig from the brandy decanter.

"Well, sir, I stand to inherit Weaselcopse Manor in Buck-inghamshire. I'm land agent for that property and some other family holdings when I'm not in town."

"Aye. It's not your income that worries me, Mr. Linsley, but your character. She has five thousand."

Five thousand?

"A year."

I almost drop my brandy glass. I'd suspected she was an heiress of some renown, but the amount had never been bandied about amongst the bachelors of the *ton*.

All this takes place against a babble of tearful girlhood reminiscences, as my mother gives Mrs. Wellesley-Clegg a run for her money.

"And what do you do in town, Mr. Linsley?"

Oh, good Lord. "I'm engaged in some philanthropic activities, Mr. Wellesley-Clegg. I am a great supporter of—" dear God, I only just remember to give its full name—"the Association for the Rescue and Succor of those in Extremis. My sister-in-law, Lady Terrant, is its president, and Miss Wellesley-Clegg the secretary."

She beams at me.

"Excellent," her papa says, a trifle dryly.

"And I do, of course, belong to White's, and attend the theater and so on. My life is not totally without amusement."

I think he believes me for one wonderful moment.

"Aye, Mr. Linsley. It is a pity you could not continue in your army career."

Oh, sod. "Indeed, yes."

"You were wounded and resigned your commission with full honors, I believe."

"Something of the sort."

He gives me a long, thoughtful stare.

I am compelled to add, "It is in fact the complete opposite, sir."

His shoulders shake and a strange wheezing sound comes from him.

At first I am alarmed, fearing he suffers from some sort of fit, before I realize he is laughing. Thank God.

"I'm most dreadfully sorry about the statue, sir. I shall of course replace it."

"Oh, aye. The statue. To tell the truth, Linsley, I never cared that much for it." He looks at the couch where the mamas, hands clasped, chatter away. The decanter is now empty. "Mrs. Wellesley-Clegg chose it for me. I'd rather hoped for something more classical, you know . . ." He makes a vague, chest-level cupping gesture.

"Indeed, you may rely on my taste and discretion, sir. I believe I can find something to complement the most elegant architecture of your home."

We shake hands.

"There is one more thing, Mr. Wellesley-Clegg. Your daughter is young and has charming high spirits. I should not like the announcement of our engagement to restrict her enjoyment of the season, which has hardly yet begun. I am not a jealous man, sir. I do not expect her to hang on my arm while London's amusements pass her by. If you are willing, let us keep this within our respective families for the moment and call the banns at season's end. With the reunion of Mrs. Wellesley-Clegg and the Dowager Countess, our families will have plenty of opportunity to meet."

"That's most generous of you, Linsley. I'd like my little girl to enjoy herself while she can." He heaves a sentimental sigh. "It's most thoughtful of you to let me keep her to myself for a few months more."

I have a sneaking suspicion that we are now humbugging each other mightily, but grip his hand in a manly, honest fashion.

The drawing-room door opens again to reveal a sight that makes me blink. For a time, after my precipitous descent from the colonel's balcony, I saw double, and this is what

I see now. Two girls a few years younger than Philomena, with ink-stained fingers and unnerving stares, stand in the doorway. It is only when one stands on one leg like a stork and the other scratches her head that I realize I am seeing two separate people.

"And these are my youngest," cries Mrs. Wellesley-Clegg. "Come here my dears and make your curtsies to the Dowager Countess of Terrant are they not sweet girls Lydia has the blue ribbon and Charlotte the green it is how we tell them apart—"

"I beg your pardon, Mama," my Philomena says. "They have changed ribbons again."

"Oh, indeed yes it is Lydia in green and Charlotte with the blue they are the clever ones in the family of course and I always say that Diana is the beauty now my dears will you not tell us what you have learned in the schoolroom today—"

"You should be grateful, madam, that Philomena has both beauty and wit in abundance." Where the devil did that come from? I sound like my brother. I don't even know that it's true.

Philomena smiles at me, a lovely smile like the sun rising, and I take a sip of brandy, somehow miss my mouth, and flood my neckcloth.

"And my dears you will never guess but Philly is engaged to this gentleman Mr. Linsley the Dowager Countess is his mama and you shall both be bridesmaids is that not splendid and we shall have such a fine time at the mantua makers oh I am quite overcome—"

In the tiny pause that ensues as she places one hand on her bosom in maternal pride, Mr. Wellesley-Clegg announces the announcement is to be deferred until the end of the season. Mrs. Wellesley-Clegg does not seem overly put out by the news.

The twins turn their unnerving double stare onto me.

"Why does Mr. Linsley have blue paint all over him?" says Lydia or possibly Charlotte. "And what happened to Hebe?"

The other one says, "We learned today of the Amazons. Did you know, so they could pull their bows better, they only had one—"

"Such clever girls," trills their mother. "And now you must play the pianoforte for us they have been practicing a duet together for these past few weeks and although I am only a proud mama and will say so many have commented on their accomplishments and excellent musical taste for ones so young for they are only fifteen and not yet out in society but so tall I hope they will not become too tall perhaps my dears you may wash the ink from your fingers before you play . . ."

My mama, who has apparently learned to tame Mrs. Wellesley-Clegg's conversational habits, heaves to her feet. "My dearest sweet Maria, I cannot express my happiness at seeing you again. Come to the play with us tonight, we can be cosy in our box, and talk if the acting does not distract us too much. Oh, my dear, do you remember when the dancing-master's wig fell off, and you said to me it looked like a dead squirrel, and I laughed so hard I—"

Good God, now my mother talks like her too, although breathing more frequently. They both double up, howling with laughter, and I realize the ladies are quite foxed.

"We'd best go home now, madam." I take her arm, but she

shakes me off and embraces her newfound bosom friend.

Wellesley-Clegg claps a hand on my shoulder. "And when do you inherit your property, Linsley?"

"I shall take possession very shortly, when my brother the earl learns of the engagement."

Her parents and my mother leave the room, leaving Philomena and me together. The twins, their identical heads bent over the pianoforte and some music, the other occupants of the room at that moment, ignore us.

"So you did it for the land," Philomena says.

Apparently she is deeply offended, despite the fact that I was noble enough to make the offer purely for her benefit. Why the devil does it matter? I really don't understand women. "Yes, I did. Damn it, I'm five-and-twenty, I'm tired of hanging on my brother's coattails."

"Perhaps that's all you're good for."

That stings me.

"I'm dreadfully sorry I can't take credit for an act of pure altruism, Miss Wellesley-Clegg."

"I too, Mr. Linsley." She brushes past me and runs up the stairs, leaving me feeling foolish and dishonorable and, to my great surprise, quite unhappy.

Miss Philomena Wellesley-Clegg

It is a dreadful thing to burst into tears twice in one day and over two different gentlemen, although not for the same reasons, of course. And now, in my bedchamber, where I have taken refuge with Mama and Hen, I weep without restraint.

I thought he liked me. That is the awful and embarrassing thing about it. I thought he . . . well, I did not think anyone could kiss a person in that way without liking her.

I don't mind about the land itself. It is perfectly natural for a gentleman to have his own establishment, so I understand, and indeed often I too wish to escape from my dear family, although I should miss Papa. I wish Mr. Linsley had told me, even though we had so little time in which to make our plan, which now I see is as full of holes as an old bucket. I fear Mama and Papa will be mightily hurt if ever they find out how I have deceived them.

And he was so kind, but then he became chilly and unpleasant and looked down his aristocratic nose at me and drawled. I'm used to that sort of look and drawl, when people find out we are not related to *those* Wellesleys, and they hear Mama and Papa talk, and learn about the coal mine.

That, I think, is why Papa has not bandied it about that I am worth a considerable fortune, and I understand the wisdom of it now. Even Mr. Linsley looked astonished when Papa mentioned it.

And I was unkind to him, telling him he was worthless, something I now bitterly regret.

I must break the engagement and take my chances with Elverton.

"Now, miss, don't take on so." Hen pats my arm.

"It is quite natural for her to cry upon becoming engaged why I did not stop crying for three days after Mr. Wellesley-Clegg made me an offer and then for the next two days after I accepted and he took me for a walk in the orchard and all was well Philly you will spoil your looks for tonight and Mr. Linsley will be put out goodness there she goes again . . ." Mama stops. "Dear me, what was I about to say?"

Hen and I stare at her in astonishment.

"I . . . Tired." Mama falls onto my bed and almost immediately lets loose a snore.

"It's been too much for her, poor lady," Hen says.

I think the brandy decanter was too much for her.

Hen removes Mama's shoes. "You'll be wanting your own maid now you're engaged."

"Oh, no, Hen, I do not want to lose you!" I wail.

"Now, miss, you're used to having your old Hen around, but I'm your mama's maid, and you'll be going out more now you're out in society and engaged. I have a lot of work to do to get Miss Lydia and Miss Charlotte ready, for they'll be next and sooner than we thought, maybe even this season. Besides, you'll be part of a grand family and need someone who knows about fashion and so on, for I'm just a country girl."

"Oh, Hen," I blubber. "Stay with me. I beg you. I'll give you my pink satin gown with the blue trim you admire so."

"Certainly not, miss, thank you all the same. I'd look like mutton dressed as lamb. Besides, you should wear that tonight."

"I don't want to go! I have a headache!" Oh heavens, it is like being an infant again.

Hen pushes Mama to one side of the bed and unhooks my ruined yellow gown. "You have a nice rest, miss, and you'll feel better when you wake up. Why, Mr. Linsley is deep in love, it's plain to see, and so handsome, and I don't believe half the gossip I've heard about him. He's not very tall, but that hardly matters for you're such a little thing. I fear this gown is beyond help, miss, though there's a good enough length on the back we can save." As she speaks she unlaces my stays while I snuffle and whimper in a most unbecoming way.

I let Hen rub my back for a while, singing about burning flesh of sinners in eternal fire, one of the hymns I remember well from when I was very young. Then she tiptoes out to leave us alone.

I find it most comforting to lie on my bed in the darkened room with someone for company, particularly as Mama has stopped snoring and does not talk. I have slept alone, elevated to the status of eldest daughter when Diana left to marry, some three years now. Sometimes it is lonely. I suppose that is why married couples, or at least the ones who get on, like to share a bed, for reasons other than the obvious ones related to matrimony. It is pleasant to have someone warm and comforting, who can make you laugh and hear your secrets there next to you.

I snuggle up to Mama, and think how strange it is to feel like a baby again when you take a step forward in your life—even though it is not a real engagement, of course. But I do not doubt that a real engagement will take place soon. I am pretty and clever, I have excellent taste in bonnets, and I can do all the things young ladies have to know to attract a husband reasonably well. I am of a practical nature and can run a household too, and I like babies. Even ones who drool and spit up, and put their fingers up their little noses, or beads, as James did once.

And there is the five thousand pounds a year.

Mr. Linsley will be sorry that he treated me so.

I have not slept with Mama since I was a little girl and when I wake I shall be grown up again and not blubber so, not even these hot, comforting tears which slide down my face and into my hair.

When I wake, I shall be a calm and rational woman, not this weepy child. And I have a great many things to do this night and while shopping tomorrow, viz:

1. Make note of what *ton* wears so can find similar cloth and advise milliner.

2. Look for bonnet to go with blue pelisse.

3. Ribbon to retrim bonnet bought yesterday. Pink?

4. Stockings.

5. Mrs. Plumley's lotion to remove freckles etc.

6. Laugh gaily in front of Mr. Linsley to show him how much I enjoy myself.

7. Bonnet to go with hideous moss-green gown should never have bought.

8. Contrasting ribbon to trim above gown so it does not look so much like a bog.

9. Trim for remainder of yellow muslin so Hen can make into sleeves.

10. Flirt with other gentlemen as much as possible.

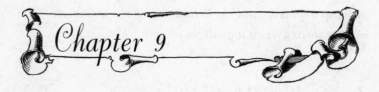

Chapter 9

Mr. Inigo Linsley

Madam,

I do not deserve the censure you have heaped upon me. Consider that you are so depraved as to accept from gentlemen you barely know offers of engagement in water-closets and

Dear Miss Wellesley-Clegg,

Despite the offense you caused me today when you slandered my person, I shall deign to forgive you, as you come from Trade and cannot

My dear Miss Wellesley-Clegg,

I shall forgive you for your impertinence towards me this afternoon, for a mere woman cannot be expected to understand the delicacies of the responsibilities thrust upon a gentleman

Dearest Miss Wellesley-Clegg,

It is indeed regrettable that I may have caused you inadvertent distress when I revealed my

Dear Philomena,

I do not wish to injure your maidenly modesty further by addressing you so, and regret deeply any indelicacy I may have shown when

Dearest Philomena,

Say I may call you thus. I cannot forget the look on your face, the contempt in your eyes, and I am to blame

Sweet Philomena,

Forgive me. I am a callous brute and you the gentlest and most lovely of women

Philomena,

*Sweet beautiful Philomena, forgive me for the
hurt I inflicted upon you so unthinkingly. I cannot eat for thinking of you, and were it not but three
hours since we parted, I am sure I should toss rest-
less all night on a bed of agony.*
~~*I to*~~

My damned neckcloth will not tie properly, and I hurl
five of them to the floor before I am satisfied. I hesitate
mightily over which pin to wear—the sapphire, so I am
told, complements my eyes wonderfully, but it seems
vulgar to wear a gift from another woman, even if I am
not really engaged. The diamond is too ostentatious. The
ruby, I always suspect, looks like a shaving accident. I
send my valet to borrow one from Pudgebum, and he
returns with a pearl pin, which I feel reflects my newfound status as a sober, industrious, and engaged country
gentleman.

I meet my sister-in-law in the drawing-room before we
leave.

"Inigo!" she cries, clasping my hands in hers. "I am so
happy for you, my dear. Oh, how I wish we could tell
the world! I cannot tell you how I admire your delicacy
in letting Philomena enjoy her season, for she has seen
so little of pleasure, stuck in that dreadful house in Lancashire, or at least however much is left of it now. But is
something wrong?"

"No, no." I hasten to reassure her. "I fear . . . I may have
offended Philomena."

"Already?" She rolls her eyes in disgust.

"Yes, I . . ." For one moment I'm tempted to reveal all to Julia, who has always had a soft spot for me, but, coward that I am, I am reluctant to lose my one ally in the family.

"I suppose she has heard about your little indiscretion."

"No. Not yet."

"I shall not say a word, Inigo, but you know you must tell Philomena of the matter. She is a kind and forgiving person, and if she truly loves you, I am convinced all will be well."

"Yes, of course."

At that moment, my mother and Pudgebum join us, and we all pack into our carriage and set off for the theater.

Philomena and Mr. and Mrs. Wellesley-Clegg are already there (the strange twins, not yet being out in society, are at home), in the box of her great-aunt Lady Rowbotham. My mother, who has previously claimed the late Sir Harold Rowbotham must have kept a very good class of drapery shop before achieving his knighthood, now greets her with the greatest of affability. Then the former Maria Cutting and Betsy Wormworth resume their giggling exchange of girlish secrets behind their fans.

Julia and Pudgebum invite Philomena and her papa to join us in our box, a quite natural thing for friends to do, and it is entirely coincidental that I am there too.

I am tongue-tied.

Philomena looked pretty the evening I lured her onto the terrace and kissed her, the same evening she disconcerted me highly by making a grab at my breeches; it was entirely innocent, I am fairly sure of it. But tonight—well, I am most mightily relieved to see her look so well, and also a little disappointed, too. To think I had imagined her weeping on her mama's shoulder at my sarcasm! Thank God I had not finished or sent any of those ridiculous letters.

She wears a pink dress with some sort of blue encrustation around the bottom, the bottom of the dress that is, whereas the top of the dress, around the bosom, is hardly there at all. (My skills with gowns are mainly in removing them, not describing them; this one, I notice, has only a few hooks at the back and would come off with very little effort.) She has a blue wreath of some sort in her hair, and her curls bounce and shine. But back to the bosom of the dress, which is fairly insubstantial, and reveals that fascinating place above the collarbone to which I am alarmingly attracted.

"Good evening, Mr. Linsley," she says, sticking her hand out.

Her hand is held sideways, poised for a frank and friendly shake.

Two can play at that game. "Miss Wellesley-Clegg." I turn her gloved hand in mine and kiss it. How I wish my lips were on her skin. "You look very well tonight."

"Thank you, sir." She settles into her chair, fiddles with her skirts so not a hint of thigh is revealed, and shoots a brilliant smile at a gentleman in the next box, a total stranger, I believe.

Flirt.

Why isn't she smiling at me like that?

I peer into her pretty bosom and sigh.

She unfurls her fan, spoils my view, and looks pointedly around the house.

"Philomena," I whisper.

"Sir? I do not believe I gave you permission to use my Christian name."

Oh ho. She's on a high horse all right.

"I'm sorry. I should have told you about the estate before."

She gives me a regal nod. Then her shoulders relax slightly, and she holds her hand out to me. "I'm sorry, too. I should not have said what I did."

"It may be true."

"No!" Her hand grips mine.

"May I call you Philomena?"

"Very well. But you are not to call me Philly. I hate it. It sounds like a horse." She withdraws her hand. "And not when others are around."

"Excellent. So we shall be alone soon?"

She rolls her eyes. "Must you flirt all the time? I think you flirt with any woman."

"I like flirting with you."

"Yes, but you don't *need* to flirt with me."

"I don't need to flirt with anyone. I like—I like being with you. I like seeing you smile." I'm in dangerous waters now.

She frowns and turns her attention to the stage. "What is this we are supposed to be watching?"

"A new comedy, I believe, although no one seems to be particularly amused by it."

On the stage a piece of scenery wobbles and an actor rushes over to prop it up.

Philomena laughs. "Mr. Linsley." She leans toward me.

"Yes?" I am careful to keep my eyes on her face.

"I do not . . . I do not feel comfortable with this arrangement. I did not realize how hard it would be to deceive Mama and Papa, and I cannot even talk to Hen about it."

"Hen?"

"Our maid. And that is another thing. I have to find a new maid; I wonder if Julia knows of anyone?"

"You can ask her tomorrow." I lean forward as Mrs. Frances Gibbons comes onto the stage wearing trousers. Old habits die hard. What a glorious sight her legs are.

The play perks up, no more scenery falls, and the actors seem to remember they are there to entertain us, not waste away time until they can get to the nearest alehouse.

I am torn between watching Philomena and Mrs. Gibbons. How pretty Philomena looks, her lips slightly parted, her eyes serious, and a fair amount of jiggling for such a small woman as she takes a deep, sentimental breath.

"Oh, she is wonderful!" Philomena exclaims at the conclusion of the song as we all applaud. "She is better than all the rest of them put together. But as I was saying, Mr. Linsley, I do not like to deceive those I love."

"Neither do I. Philomena, we'll end it now, if you like."

"But your estate . . ."

I wish I could say, hang the estate, but I cannot. Nothing is yet signed, and I cannot remain in my brother's good graces indefinitely.

She sees my hesitation. "Whom do you love, Mr. Linsley?"

I am glad she does not ask me whom I deceive, for I am so used to deception it bothers me very little.

I reply, "My brother Terrant. And my other brother George, the parson. He has a living on Terrant's estate. My niece and nephew, George's children. Julia. My nurse. My old dog, Venus." To my embarrassment I blow my nose at this point.

She looks at me with eyes full of sympathy. "Is—is she dead?"

"Yes, but I've several of her puppies."

She frowns. "I meant your nurse."

"Oh, she's lively as a cricket. And there's someone else, too . . ." Well, I have to tell her sometime, and why not now? "My son."

"You have a son?"

Miss Philomena Wellesley-Clegg

Hen was quite right to insist I wear the pink dress tonight, for it shows off my bosom mightily well. Mr. Linsley, not to mention the gentleman in the next box, the one opposite with the quizzing-glass, three gentlemen on the way into the theater, and several others who visited my great-aunt's box, have all noticed my feminine charms.

Mr. Linsley apologizes to me, which I find astonishing, for both Julia and Diana have told me that a man will never admit to be in the wrong. It is in fact quite endearing, and although I have enjoyed playing the flirt and being high and mighty with him, I unbend a little. But only a little.

He wants to call me by my Christian name! The impertinence! I love the way my name, which I do not like overmuch, sounds on his tongue. His tongue. That odd, strange, fizzing feeling returns. When he says my name, I mean.

And he gets vastly sentimental over his dead dog, and I feel quite tender toward him.

And then he mentions a Certain Matter which reminds me once again that he is of the *ton* and I am not, and I just gape at him like an idiot. I am aware, of course, as Mama has told me, that men have Needs, and that sometimes children will result. It is a matter to be treated with discretion, so I have always thought—not, of course, that Papa would ever have done such a thing; he has always been too busy with the mine and lately with the subsidence problem, and, besides, I know he loves Mama faithfully.

There was a girl at Miss Grimsley's Academy for Gentlewomen (yes, I too attended that august establishment, and I can only hope in a decade or so I will believe I enjoyed it half as much as the Dowager Countess and Mama apparently did)—who had no discernible papa, for she never talked of him. And then one very exciting day, a handsome carriage with a coat of arms drew up, and I shall never forget the look on her face, for it was her papa come to visit. He never returned. For days after she cried and none of us could comfort her. Much later I realized she was born out of wedlock, and that was why her father visited only the one time.

But I digress.

When Mr. Linsley made his announcement, I sat there dumb with astonishment.

What disconcerted me was the pride and joy on his face. It was not the boastful leer I should have expected. He seems genuinely pleased that his Needs had resulted in what, to other men, might be an inconvenience or an embarrass-ment.

"I do not shock you, I hope, Philomena?"

"Oh, no. That is, well, it is unexpected to be sure. I . . ." I wanted to say it was a good thing we were not really en-gaged, for not every woman would wish for the open accep-tance of her betrothed's b—d. It is an ugly word, to be sure.

"Ah. So that is why your mouth hangs open so."

"It does *not*!"

He casts a wary look around the box. Papa, as he tends to do when seated in a relatively quiet place (away from Mama and her chattering tongue), has fallen asleep. Ter-rant and Julia sit close together, carefully ignoring us.

"We are friends, are we not, Philomena?"

His whispered question takes me by surprise. Friends? I am not sure. We are . . . something, and I fear to explore exactly what that may be. His warm breath heats my skin but it makes me shiver.

"Allies, then? Fellow conspirators?"

"I—I suppose so."

"And you trust me?"

"I'm not sure. I don't think you are a particularly trust-worthy person."

"Ah. I asked for that, I suppose." His arm settles on the back of my chair and his fingers touch my shoulder. *My skin.*

I move away from him. It is too much like when we were in the water-closet and he made me agree to a plan of du-bious honor which already, only hours later, proves to be troublesome. Then, as now, it is his physical presence which stirs me and makes a jelly of me. However, I am a sensible woman, and not kitchen ingredients.

He stands and offers me his hand. "Miss Wellesley-Clegg, I should be honored if you would pay me the great compliment of meeting my son."

I have a thousand questions on the tip of my tongue. How old is he, who is his mother, does he love her? Instead I blurt out the silliest thing I can. "He is here?"

"Close by."

He has a son old enough to attend the play? Mr. Linsley is, I believe, five-and-twenty, which would have made him very young to become a father. There are a few children in the pit, of course, but . . .

I place my hand in his.

Julia, who has kept her eyes carefully averted from us as though she found the play interesting—Mrs. Gibbons has left the scene and it rapidly deteriorates again—offers to accompany us.

"It's all right, Julia," Mr. Linsley says. "We're paying a visit to the backstage."

"Oh. I see." She gives me a concerned look. "Are you sure, Philomena?"

"Quite sure," Mr. Linsley replies. "We shall be very discreet."

My excitement wins out over my hesitancy. "The backstage? Oh, do you think we can meet Mrs. Gibbons? I do so admire her!"

Julia looks at Terrant, who shrugs.

"Why, certainly," Mr. Linsley says. He tucks my hand into the crook of his elbow.

"Inigo . . ." Julia tugs at his other arm to whisper something in his ear.

What on earth are they about?

"Don't be a ninny, my dear," Mr. Linsley says to her, and pushes me out of the box and into the passage. "You should be glad to have such a protective friend."

"I am, indeed." So Julia knows about his child, and I think she knows something else too. I wonder if we are really going to the backstage, but realize, as Mr. Linsley leads me downstairs and through a series of discreet doors, that is indeed our destination.

It is quite exciting. We emerge into a dimly lit area, which is at the side of the stage. We can see the actors and actresses, and hear them too. One of the actors, who awaits his entry on the stage, shakes Mr. Linsley's hand, and bows and kisses mine, and he too is impressed with the cut of my pink gown.

It is dirty and dusty, and there are strange bits and pieces of scenery standing around. A large table holds items such as the dagger used in the tragedy earlier that night, and a tree in a tub, which looked quite real on the stage, but not up close.

We pass a woman, scantily clad in flesh-colored tights and gauze, and a man with a terrier in a frilly collar, as we emerge into a corridor lit with rush-lights. A well-dressed man pauses to shake Mr. Linsley's hand and ask him how he's enjoying the play.

"It's quite dreadful," Mr. Linsley says, clapping him on the shoulder. "Did you write it?"

"I fear so, sir. Yet the actors will insist on changing my lines."

"How unfortunate." Mr. Linsley does not introduce me, but steers me forward to a door marked "Ladies' Dressing Room." Some other gentlemen crowd around the door, and I am pleased to see Aylesworth and The Mad Poet there.

"'Pon my word, the divine Miss Wellesley-Clegg and the dashing Mr. Linsley," Aylesworth says. "A charming gown, my dear, but one I believe we have seen rather frequently this season."

"I like it," I say. "It is my favorite. Are you going to visit Mrs. Gibbons?"

"Ah, if only we were allowed into the inner sanctum," The Mad Poet says. "We adore her. She is a goddess."

"I thought I was, sir."

"So you are, Miss Wellesley-Clegg," Aylesworth says. "But is it not scandalous for you to be here in a gentleman's company?"

"My sister-in-law and Terrant, are here too, although I think they have been distracted." The easy delivery of Mr. Linsley's lie appalls me. He raises his hand to knock on the door.

"Oh, should we go in there? They may not be decent." I am quite shocked.

The other gentlemen snigger and some of them, but not Aylesworth and The Mad Poet who whisper together, look down my bosom.

"Go away," says someone inside, in reply to Mr. Linsley's knock. "We've told you a dozen times."

"It's Inigo Linsley."

There is a pause, and some giggling. "Very well, but the others are not to come in."

We enter a room full of women in various states of undress, maybe a dozen of them, crammed in together. The air is thick with sweat, and the room is littered with gowns, wigs, hairbrushes, pots of facepaint, and wreaths of silk flowers. It is both squalid and exciting.

"Ladies, your servant." Mr. Linsley seems very much at home here, and quite unaffected by the abundance of female flesh—a couple are down to their shifts, and one is in the act of drawing on her stockings.

He takes my hand and pulls me to the back of the room, quite the brightest area, as it is lit with beeswax candles, and where a woman in shirt and breeches sits.

It is Mrs. Gibbons!

Up close, her facepaint looks fairly hideous, and she appears smaller than she does onstage. What I thought might be a wig is her own hair, reddish, and cut fashionably short. Until she smiles at Inigo, I think her a disappointingly plain woman, after having seen her as both a dazzling beauty and a handsome young man on the stage.

"My dear, I have not seen you in an age—it must be two days at least."

He kisses her hand. "Fanny, this is Miss Philomena Wellesley-Clegg."

"I'm very pleased to meet you," I babble. "I do so like your singing although the play is dreadful, and I am so glad you are in it."

"Thank you. Do you sing, as your name would suggest, Miss Wellesley-Clegg?" Her voice is warm and throaty, with the hint of an Irish accent.

"Oh, no. Hardly at all. I do not play very well either. It is hard to do two things at once."

"I agree. It took me a long time to learn to sing and dance

together—Inigo, what are you about, under my dressing-table?"

"Where is he, Fan?" Inigo emerges, brushing dust from his coat.

"Over there. He is asleep. Please let him alone." She shrugs and looks at me. "I do not know why I bother to ask, for of course he will wake him; he always does. May I ask, are you related to *those* Wellesleys?"

"No, I'm afraid not."

"I had His Grace sniffing around my skirts once," another actress interjects.

"I, too," says another, giggling. "There was scarce enough room in here for him and his big nose."

A general ripple of hilarity runs through the room. I am shocked that they should talk of the hero of Waterloo so!

Inigo, meanwhile, rummages in a large open chest near-by and gives a cry of triumph. "Ah, here he is. My little boy!"

Mr. Linsley turns, a baby of about six months in his arms, who wrinkles up his face and gives a loud squawk of protest at his rude awakening. There is no doubt whose child he is, with that curly black hair, and when he looks at Mr. Linsley and his initial suspicion fades, he has a similar wide smile, *sans* teeth of course.

"Dadadada!" The baby exclaims.

"He's talking! You never told me, Fanny."

"Oh, don't be so foolish."

"But he said Dada."

Mrs. Gibbons rolls her eyes. "Did you ever see a man so besotted with a baby, Miss Wellesley-Clegg?"

"I think he needs changing," Inigo announces.

"Oh, pray do the honors." She pushes a chair towards me. "Miss Wellesley-Clegg, please sit. Inigo, do not use the blue velvet to change him on. It is my costume for the tragedy."

"It stinks already."

"The manager will fine me if it's soiled." She shakes her head. "At least put something beneath him."

The other actresses gather around as women will when a baby is undressed, and coo and admire him.

"What a sweet little doodle," one comments. "Like a little thimble, bless him."

A *doodle*? That is a word I never thought to hear spoken in company, and indeed have only heard from Diana.

"He's a lovely baby," I finally manage to say, afraid that I sit there like a tongue-tied fool. And indeed, he is a charming baby. But I am shocked that Mr. Linsley apparently forgot to tell me his mother would be present, and who she was. "What is his name?"

"Will. After Shakespeare. William Henry Gibbons." Mr. Linsley tickles his son's belly. "Say Dada again."

The baby, clutching both feet in his hands, obliges with a stream of adorable infant gibberish, beaming all the while.

"Miss Wellesley-Clegg?" Mrs. Gibbons looks at me with concern. "I am afraid this—myself and the baby—may have come as somewhat of a surprise to you."

I am trying with all my heart to dislike her, although I cannot deny the tumult of emotions I feel. He should have warned me, of course. Once again I struggle for words. "No, I am . . . well, there were plenty of hints, and he did tell me of Will, but . . ."

"Believe me, Miss Wellesley-Clegg, I am delighted to make

your acquaintance, although I am aware of the impropriety of this meeting. I only wish Mr. Linsley was too."

"Yes, but . . ." Strangely enough, this has the effect of making me want to defend him.

There is a burst of laughter from the actresses, and Inigo rears to his feet.

"D—n it, your son has p—d on me!"

"Well, so he will if he becomes cold. You should know better." She turns to me. "You will see how suddenly Will is *my* son if he does something of which his papa disapproves."

Amidst much giggling from the actresses, Mr. Linsley wipes off his coat with a towel and sets to work pinning the baby into a clean napkin.

I am dumbfounded. Does Mr. Linsley intend to set up house with his mistress—or former mistress, although I am not so sure of that—at Weaselcopse Manor (which is an exceedingly silly name, now I think of it)? And does Mrs. Gibbons know of our false engagement? And what, I wonder, does Mr. Gibbons, wherever he may be, think of his wife's indiscretion?

Mr. Linsley plops Will onto my lap. "Is he not a fine boy?"

But he is. He shoots his little arms and legs out like a starfish, chuckling and cooing, with a wide grin on his face. He is warm and squirmy and altogether adorable.

Mrs. Gibbons reaches below her shirt to unwind a wide strip of cloth. "I have to flatten myself to make a convincing boy," she explains, gathering the cloth in her hands and bundling it onto her dressing table. She holds out her arms to the baby. "Come here, my love."

I pass Will to her, and we both laugh as he opens and

shuts his mouth like a little fish, before diving onto his mother's breast with a loud smacking grunt. It's a strange situation, to be sure, a woman in a man's clothes suckling a baby while her lover and his alleged fiancée look on.

"As soon as Terrant and I have the papers signed, I'll go down to the country and make sure the cottage is in fit state," Mr. Linsley says. "I may have to have some work done on the chimney, but you'll find it snug and comfortable. It's but a half mile from the Manor, so I'll walk over often to see you."

"If you ever plan to marry, you sad rake," Mrs. Gibbons says, "it will have to be to an exceptional woman who would tolerate your mistress beneath her nose. Don't you agree, Miss Wellesley-Clegg?"

Mr. Linsley winks at me and I want to slap him.

Mistress. She did not say *former* mistress.

I endeavor to change the subject. My gaze falls upon a most handsome bonnet standing on Mrs. Gibbons' dressing-table, and I remark upon it.

"Oh, yes, that is new, but now I wonder about the velvet ribbon. Do you think I should retrim it with a satin?"

"Possibly, but that tawny color is very good. Is it from Mrs. Merriweather's shop?"

"Why, indeed, yes. I admire her work greatly. I see you are a connoisseur of bonnets, Miss Wellesley-Clegg. They are a great source of pleasure to me."

"As they are to Miss Wellesley-Clegg. The two of you should go shopping together," Mr. Linsley says.

"Absolutely not!" Mrs. Gibbons glares at him. "Have you no sense of propriety at all, sir?" She glances at me. "Un-

der different circumstances, of course, I should be only too
pleased."

"If you wish to be improper, I could come too. I could
look after Will." Inigo, I am convinced, is now trying to
shock us both.

"No," we both say together, and I am glad she agrees with
me.

There's a rap on the door. "Mrs. Gibbons? Five minutes,
if you please."

"I'll take him while you go onstage," Mr. Linsley offers.

"No, you may not, for he's dropping off to sleep, and
you'll only wake him to play with him." She looks at me
with a shy smile. "Miss Wellesley-Clegg, if you will, please
put him down to sleep in the costume chest again."

In my arms, Will smacks his lips and makes sleepy, sucking movements, his body warm and limp. He gives a brief
whimper of protest when I lay him down in the chest, before flinging his balled fists up beside his head and falling
deeply asleep.

"My little man," Mr. Linsley says softly and leans to kiss
him. "I do so long to teach him to play cricket."

Now transformed again into a young man, Fanny smiles
at us both and swaggers toward the door. I swear she is a
whole head taller. She is certainly an inch or so taller than
Mr. Linsley, who catches her hand in his as she passes to
kiss it.

I am purely astonished to have seen the worldly Mr. Linsley dandle a baby, and there's something else I feel which
shames me—envy. I wish Will was my baby, and I wish I
had the friendly ease with someone that Mr. Linsley and

Mrs. Gibbons enjoy. They use first names, there is an affectionate intimacy between them, and it reminds me—dear heavens, it reminds me of my own mama and papa.

But even though little Will is delightful, I wish I had not been told of him, or of his mother.

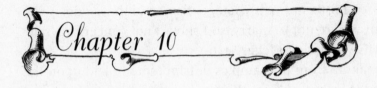

Chapter 10

Miss Philomena Wellesley-Clegg

By an extraordinary coincidence I visit Mrs. Merriweather's shop the next day.

Of course I do not go there on the chance that I might meet Mrs. Gibbons and particularly not to meet Mr. Linsley escorting his mistress—or former mistress; I really am not sure of the relationship between them at present. I wonder that he can afford to keep a mistress, or indeed how he has had the time, while acting as Terrant's land agent. Of course, as I have heard from several women, quite often begetting a child takes very little time at all—*blink and you've missed it*, as I once heard one of Mama's friends complain.

But if Mr. Linsley were to marry an heiress—and this is a thought that makes me most uncomfortable—he could keep a dozen mistresses. It is what gentlemen of the *ton* do.

But we are not to marry, so I should not concern myself.

"Miss Wellesley-Clegg?"

I look up from the samples of trim that are laid upon the counter for my perusal (I must admit I have barely looked at them, as distracted as I find myself today).

I see a well-dressed, ladylike woman, with nothing remarkable about her save her eyes and that perfectly splendid bonnet I admired last night. If it were not for the bonnet, I don't believe I should have recognized her.

"Why, Mrs. Gibbons!" My voice, which unlike hers is not low and melodious in the best of circumstances, comes out as a sort of squawk. I look over my shoulder to see if Hen lurks. No, she is sitting with her nose buried deep in a fashion paper.

"This is somewhat awkward," Mrs. Gibbons says. "I'll leave directly."

"Oh, no. No. I was about to leave myself."

"Oh, please, not on my account."

We stand and stare at each other.

"Mr. Linsley—" We both speak the same words simultaneously.

Hen looks up, frowns, and returns to her fashion paper.

"Miss Wellesley-Clegg, you should not be seen with me," Mrs. Gibbons says with a smile that denies the harshness of her words.

"Yes, but . . . I have no right to ask you to leave and I shall not. It is unjust. Besides, I have serious business to which I must attend." I gesture to the pile of ribbon and trim samples.

"Of course." She hesitates. "I wonder . . . may I possibly ask your advice?"

For one hideous moment I fear she is about to ask me something relating to Mr. Linsley.

"I have a velvet spenser—it is new, and now I realize I have no bonnet to match." She pulls a scrap from her reticule. "The color, as you can see, is somewhat unusual, a cross between blue and green. I should welcome another pair of eyes and some advice."

"I should be honored," I say, still not altogether comfortable in her presence.

"And if someone you know comes into the shop, I shall be discreet."

"Mrs. Gibbons, I . . ." I stumble to a halt. This seems so grossly unfair, but I cannot think how to put it into words. If it were not blasphemous, I should imagine myself a sort of Saint Peter denying Mrs. Gibbons ere the cock crew three times. "It is not your fault you had Mr. Linsley's baby."

She smiles, but in a kind way, not at the idiocy of my comment. "It's most kind of you to say so, Miss Wellesley-Clegg, but I must assume half the blame."

Unless of course she blinked and missed the moment, but somehow I do not think a woman could be anything but very aware of such an activity with Mr. Linsley.

Determined to put such indecent thoughts from my mind, I apply myself to the matter at hand. Although at first we are still shy and formal with each other, we find our taste in bonnets similar and our conversation becomes easier. We spend an hour or so trying on bonnets and looking at various trimmings—she has an excellent eye for color and wears a most elegant rust-colored gown and pelisse that match her bonnet exactly. She suggests a bright blue, a color I should have not considered myself, for the contrast to the moss-green gown, which appears to me more dingy than ever. To my great pleasure, I order a bonnet with ostrich feathers dyed the same bright blue and ribbons in peach, a color far more suited to me, and I am most excited, for it will look excellent with my cream pelisse. Papa will be so pleased that I save money.

To match her spenser, we find a handsome sea-green velvet that I think will look excellent with her complexion, and a deep pink velvet ribbon.

After buying various trims, gloves, stockings, and other things, I send Hen home in a hackney with my parcels, and Fanny—for we have decided we must use our Christian names—and I retire to Gunter's Tea Shop for ices.

"Ah, this is very pleasant," Fanny says. "Bonnets and ices—I can think of nothing better. I am glad Mr. Linsley is not with us, for he would have only been bored and flirted abominably with the milliners to amuse himself. How are you enjoying London, Philomena?"

"Quite well. I have had my presentation at court and Almack's, which is a dreadfully boring place. And Mama and Papa plan a coming-out ball for me soon."

"Forgive me if I am forward, but are you and Mr. Linsley . . . ?" So she has been wondering about it too.

"We are not—that is . . ." I stumble to a halt.

"Forgive me. I did not mean to intrude."

"Not at all. It is rather complicated." I feel as awkward and guilty as I would if trying to explain it to Mama and Papa, or Julia. "Has Mr. Linsley said anything of it?"

"He told me he met an adorable woman about whom he thinks far too much," Fanny says. "I imagine that is you."

"I suppose so." For some reason this makes me feel miserable.

"And it's about time. He should marry." She takes a spoonful of ice in a thoughtful way. "It will be good for him. He lacks purpose, as you doubtless know, and he should like to have more children."

"How is Will?" I am glad to change the subject. "He is a lovely baby."

"Well, of course I'd agree with you. I think he has a tooth coming in; he drools and chews at everything. Did Mr. Linsley tell you he has already bought him a cricket bat?"

We both laugh, and I ask her about her career in the theater.

"According to my mama I was born backstage in the Theater Royal, Dublin," Fanny tells me. "She also said she went out straight after for the last act of *Romeo and Juliet*, but I do not quite believe that. I do remember sleeping in the dressing-room, as Will does, when I was little, and then playing the Indian child in *Midsummer Night's Dream* when I was about three. And I have been on the stage, in Dublin first, and then in various theaters in England, ever since."

"Do you enjoy it?"

"It's my trade." She shrugs. "I'm no longer young. There are prettier and very ambitious women who wait to take my place on the stage. I intend to retire, or at least retire mostly, when I choose, and not when I am forced out. Besides, I wish to spend time with my son as he grows. I should like to raise him in the country, and close to his father." She draws a watch from her reticule. "Heavens, I must go home. Philomena, this has been a pleasure indeed."

I insist on taking her home in the carriage, although she resists at first, saying she can take a hackney. She lives in a small house in Soho, and does not ask me in, to my disappointment, for I should like to see Will again.

On the ride home I am not altogether happy, despite a most satisfactory shopping trip and the company of my new friend. I should so like to have confided in Fanny, and I am impressed that Mr. Linsley has not told her our engagement is false. She is astute enough, however, to know that not all is as it should be.

I drive to Diana's house for luncheon and find her in excellent health, although she assures me had I arrived half an hour earlier, I would have found her a miserable, sick wretch.

"Now, tell me all about Mr. Linsley!" she cries. "How sudden it has been! When did he make the offer? Was it when you waltzed together?"

"No, it was the next day, in the water-closet."

"Oh. How . . ." She searches for a word. "Precipitate."

"Indeed, yes. Oh, Di, I must tell you of the bonnet I bought today . . ." As I launch into a description of the splendor of the new hat she looks at me, with her brow creased.

". . . And Fanny said it would suit me above all things. She bought a . . ."

"Fanny?"

"Yes, she is a new friend."

"Oh." My sister bites her lip. "Fanny who?"

"Fanny Gibbons."

"Philly, she's Mr. Linsley's mistress. You cannot go shopping with her!"

I toss my head, feeling daring and slightly scandalous. "We met by chance. She has excellent taste in bonnets. And I like her."

"Philly." Diana takes my hand and gazes at me with sorrowful eyes. "She had a child by him. Did you know that?"

"Yes, he's a lovely baby. Almost as nice as James," I add diplomatically, for I know it is more than likely that Will, when he is two, will also become a little monster. "And I think it very good of Mr. Linsley to support his child."

"Indeed. I wonder whether you will think so when you have your own children, and his b—d lords it over them."

"I . . . That is not fair, Di!" Not for the first time in our lives I am quite angry at my sister, but this time I cannot work out why. I shall not marry Mr. Linsley, and so how he treats his children, legitimate or otherwise, is none of my concern.

"And what about poor Tom Darrowby?" my sister, who is in a dreadfully unpleasant mood, asks.

"He does not know?" I had rather hoped my sister would have told him, to my shame, because otherwise that duty falls to me.

"No, he does not. I know we agreed to keep this within our families, but he is almost like a brother to us, and you should tell him."

How I loathe my sister when she takes a high moral stance. It is even worse when I know she is right.

"Very well." I slam my dessert spoon down onto the table. "I shall tell him now."

I stamp upstairs to Tom's office, in a dreadful mood. Of course I should have thought of this myself. I should not treat Tom so shabbily; he is my friend. He will be happy that I am engaged—I think. I pause outside the door. It is a low-ceilinged room, quite small, and most of the space is taken up with a large desk, at which Tom sits. He wears his spectacles, and he is surrounded by piles of paper as his pen scratches away. At his elbow stands a pewter mug and a plate of bread and cheese. As I watch, he stops, takes a draught from the mug, and then sees me and stands, tucking his spectacles into his waistcoat pocket.

"Why, Philomena, this is a pleasant surprise! Come in, do." He offers me a chair. "You may share my beer, if you like."

This is a joke between us, after I drank some of the Christmas wassail cup, and became sick when I was about ten years of age. I shake my head, no, and refuse his bread and cheese also.

"You look very serious," he says. "Is everything well?"

"Oh, yes. Yes, thank you. What keeps you so busy?"

"Merely some letters for Mr. Pullen. It is nothing important, I assure you, and I'm glad to have an interruption."

He does indeed look pleased to see me, even after our

most recent and uncomfortable encounter. I sit on his chair, and he perches on the edge of his desk, one foot swinging.

There is no easy way to do it. "I'm engaged," I announce.

His foot halts in mid-swing. "I should congratulate you, Miss Wellesley-Clegg. And who is the lucky gentleman?"

"Mr. Inigo Linsley. But we are to keep it secret."

He stands and walks over to the window, gazing out at the traffic below. "Indeed. I suppose his family do not know?"

"Oh, no, no, it is nothing of the sort. The Dowager Countess and my mother, it appears, were friends at school, and they are most fond of each other. It is only that we do not wish to make an announcement until the end of the season."

"I see."

"I'm very happy," I mumble, wishing I could tell him, anyone, of the truth of the matter.

"And is he desperately in love with you?"

"Of course he is. We are engaged! Don't be obtuse, Tom."

"Listen, Philly, he's *ton*. His family are devilish proud, he's as poor as a church mouse and under their thumb, and of course he's looking for an heiress to snap up."

"I don't think—"

"And it's common knowledge he keeps a mistress, some lightskirt—"

"She is not a lightskirt. She is very amiable—"

"You've met her?" He shakes his head. "Oh, Philly, Philly, you're in way over your head. He's charming, a good enough fellow, but feckless and unscrupulous. He'll squander your fortune, he'll—"

"Stop it, Tom!"

"Philly," he says quite quietly, and takes my hand. To my surprise, he draws off my glove and kisses my fingers.

"Tom!" It is not the exciting sort of sizzle Mr. Linsley produces, but there is something there—tenderness, affection, and a sort of sadness, too, all from his lips on my fingers. "You haven't done that since I slammed my finger in the stable door when I was eight."

"I know."

I wrench my hand back, startled by the expression on his face. "And that was your fault. If you and Robert had not scuffled in the doorway I should not have been hurt."

"I don't want to see you hurt again, Philly, your fingers or your heart."

If only it had been Tom who offered me a false engagement. But he is too true and honest a man to do such a thing, and I am ashamed again at how I deceive those I love. I am also aware that I am becoming more skilled at deception, and can only attribute it to Mr. Linsley's influence.

"I'd best go, Tom, Mr. Darrowby, I mean."

"Very well." He bows and offers me my glove back.

I fumble my hand into it, suddenly clumsy, and run from his office, longing to be alone, or at least away from him.

On the way home in the carriage, I make a list of good reasons why I should not marry Mr. Linsley, even if circumstances were different, which they will never be:

1. He is not quite tall enough.

2. His mama is a snob, although exceedingly affable of late.

3. Although as Mama says, men have Needs, it was wrong of him to have a child out of wedlock.

4. He lacks direction, as Fanny says, and I do not see why marriage should change that; and what if Tom says is true, that he is feckless and wicked?

5. He is a dreadful flirt.

6. He looked at my bosom overmuch at the theater.

7. He has called me a ninny.

8. His proposal, which was not really a proposal at all, was in a most indelicate location.

9. I become exceedingly silly and clumsy when he is near me.

10. His kisses make me feel very peculiar indeed, and I should wish to feel only comfortable with my husband, not all hot and shivery and indecent.

It is quite clear to me that I must find a husband as soon as possible. But before I do, I should like Mr. Linsley to kiss me one more time. A few last moments of hot shivery indecency would not be so unwelcome.

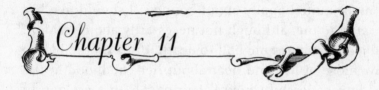

Chapter 11

Mr. Inigo Linsley

I do my duty. At White's, I let slip a rumor about Miss Wellesley-Clegg's surprising fortune, to interest a wider field of gentlemen in her.

I hate to do it. It will open her up to the advances of feck-less fortune-hunters, but it is my job to protect her from them. Elverton, to my relief, has gone back to his estate in Staffordshire, doubtless to soothe his damaged heart in the company of his Guernsey cow. I was afraid he might spread news of the false engagement, but it is not so.

I am concerned that Philomena suffers from not being able to confide in a soul about our arrangement. In fact, the only person in whom she can confide is me.

In a word, she is my responsibility, as much as the up-keep of the land and the welfare of the tenants are at Weaselcopse, and I find that I quite like the idea of looking after her. I suspect she would have prattled on to Fanny last night quite happily about bonnets; I should like her to prattle to me, although not necessarily about fashion, a subject that bores me half to death. But I should like to know more of her and hear about her childhood in the subsiding Lancashire house. I want her to trust me, to tell me secrets.

I want to tell her mine, although I have already, with great indelicacy, revealed the existence of my son and former mistress.

I want to see her again.

Damnation.

My dear Miss Wellesley-Clegg,

I should be most honored if you accompany me on horseback in Hyde Park this afternoon at four. Terrant and his lady will come with us to preserve decencies.

I am, madam,
your most faithful servant,
Inigo Linsley

Dear Mr. Linsley,

I am greatly honored but fear I must decline as I do not keep a horse.

Yours truly,
Philomena Wellesley-Clegg

Dear Miss Wellesley-Clegg,

I shall provide a suitable mount, you ninny.

J.L.

Dear Mr. Linsley,

Neither do I own a riding-habit.

P.W.C.

Philomena,

You run our footmen ragged. Julia is pleased to send with this note a habit she believes will fit, and says if it is a trifle too long, it is no great matter. Also boots and a hat. I believe you may own gloves and other things. If there is anything else you need,

I fear you will have to do without, as I look forward to arriving shortly after you receive this letter.

J.L.

Miss Philomena Wellesley-Clegg

I am to ride in the Park at the most fashionable time of day! I am truly one of the *ton* now, and must practice looking haughty and bored. And I look forward to riding again—it feels an age since I ambled around the grounds of our house on dear old Strawberry.

Papa is most upset to receive a letter from Robert, reporting a fissure that opened in the garden near the asparagus bed, taking with it the third gardener. Fortunately, he was not injured, as one of the kichen maids, who was with him at the time, nobly removed her petticoat to use as a rope. They both called for help and poor John was hauled out, although somehow in the excitement he had lost his breeches. How frightened they must have been!

The main house holds steady for the moment.

Julia's habit fits well enough and looks most becoming after Hen stitches me into it around the bosom, warning me not to exert myself, for I will burst it. It is a dark red, which I think makes me look interesting. The boots are a little too big, but I wear two pairs of stockings.

And I shall see Mr. Linsley again! And Julia and Terrant, of course.

"They are here," Mama reports, and follows behind me,

lifting the skirts of the habit as though it were a train. She continues, as we proceed down the stairs and into the hall, "Now pray remember Philly you are not openly engaged so you must not show partiality in public to Mr. Linsley indeed I was quite shocked to see you and he disappeared somewhere together last night you must learn to be more discreet for people will talk and I cannot have anything upset the planning for your coming-out ball unless of course your papa has to return home if an important part of the house subsides which I fear is all too likely though I am glad the asparagus was mostly spared for it is a food I do enjoy greatly and Robert will send the first crop to us here in town my dear what do you think of a Chinese theme for the ball I do not believe it has been done yet this season I must talk to my dearest Betsy about it oh good afternoon my dear Mr. Linsley to be sure what a fine pair you and my sweet Philly make—"

"Your servant, madam." I see that Mr. Linsley is learning the art of intercepting Mama's flow of words. "Good afternoon, Miss Wellesley-Clegg."

"Good afternoon, Mr. Linsley." Naturally, I drop my gloves.

We step back to avoid damage to our heads, remembering what happened the last time I dropped something, and we both reached for it, and our footman intervenes to pick them up and hand them to me. I put them on, foolishly trying to cram my right hand into my left glove, and hope Mr. Linsley does not notice.

I take his arm and we go outside, where Julia and Terrant are on horseback, and a groom holds the reins of two horses.

We exchange greetings, and I thank Julia for the loan of the habit.

"This is Blaze," Mr. Linsley says, slapping the neck of the one with the sidesaddle, a most pretty chestnut, who does indeed have a white blaze on its face.

"Oh, she's so pretty." I stroke the horse's glossy skin.

He grins. "It's a gelding, Philomena."

"Oh, to be sure." I restrain myself from ducking to view the animal's belly.

"Give me your foot. No, the other one." He tosses me into the air and onto the saddle. I never realized how strong he was! "I'll shorten the stirrup leather for you."

I want to touch his hair as he stands next to me, his head at the level of my knee. I remember how it felt when he kissed me. I must admit it makes me feel quite peculiar as he pushes the woollen fabric of the habit aside.

He looks up at me and grins again. Does he know what I am thinking?

He busies himself with the stirrup leather. It does seem to take rather a long time, and I'm not sure he needs to press his shoulder so against my leg.

"There. That should suffice." The wicked man slips his hand to the leg crooked around the horn of the sidesaddle and tickles me behind my knee, beneath both stockings. Oh, the shame!

I release a strange squeaking sound and Blaze shakes his mane.

"He's quite fresh." Mr. Linsley winks at me. "You'll enjoy him."

"Thank you," I say, at a loss for words.

Blaze shifts and idles beneath me. This is nothing like dear Strawberry, who tends to sleep if she stands for any length of time. The thought strikes me that the energy and strength of this horse remind me of Mr. Linsley, which is quite indecent since I have good reason to believe him intact in all ways. Besides, I am perched on top of this large animal, and . . . I decide not to pursue these disturbing thoughts.

He, meanwhile, takes the reins of the other horse and vaults into the saddle without use of the stirrups.

"He is such a show-off," Julia murmurs to me. "He is quite wonderfully in love with you, Philomena."

"I don't . . ." But at that moment the groom steps away, and we all move forward, Inigo's horse (a mare, I take note) circling and then dancing sideways as he reins her in. He looks very well indeed on horseback, and I should like to watch him, but have to concentrate on Blaze, who seems inclined to push forward ahead of the others.

I pull him back, pleased that he obeys.

"Is everything well between you?" Julia asks.

"Oh, yes." Then I realize to what she refers. "Yes, I met Mrs. Gibbons, and she is very charming. And the baby is quite delightful."

"I have not met either," Julia says. "It is something we do not talk much about in the family. Inigo is quite open, possibly too much so, about the matter. I was afraid you would break off the engagement."

"Not at all." I do store the idea in my mind as a reason I can give Julia when I end the engagement, although why I should wait a matter of weeks before deciding to do so seems absurd.

She adds, to my discomfiture, "I am most glad of it. I think it admirable he chooses to support his child, for many gentlemen would refuse the responsibility. And, of course, his wife should feel comfortable with the arrangement."

Oh, I do not like this at all. I might lose Julia as my friend, and it is she who took pity on me at boarding-school and more recently has guided me through the maze of my entrée into society. I feel I betray her.

We clatter through the streets and into the Park, where the most fashionable of all—and I am now one of them— parade in open carriages or on horseback. Mr. Linsley turns to smile at me, and I smile back.

One of the advantages of being on horseback is that we can weave in and out of the carriages, or break away to canter beside the road. I see several people I recognize, including one of the gentlemen who looked into my bosom last night, and he has the impertinence to raise his hat to me. Shocking! We have not even been introduced.

"Miss Wellesley-Clegg, would you care to ride with me?" Mr. Linsley reins in his mare and gestures to me.

"Please do," Julia says. "Blaze needs the exercise. Do not worry about people talking. You should take every opportunity to snatch these moments alone with Inigo."

"Be careful, Inigo," Terrant calls to his brother, and then to me, says, "He is rather a reckless rider, Miss Philomena, even in Hyde Park. Do not follow him unless you wish."

"Do not concern yourself, sir," I say, only too aware that beneath me Blaze seems to be coiling himself into a tight spring, and snorts and sidles. He plunges forward after Mr. Linsley's mare and I make a quick grab at the pommel to right myself.

Ahead of us is a wide expanse of parkland, grass dotted with widely-spaced trees. A few other riders canter sedately there.

Blaze shakes his head and gives a loud snort.

"Steady, boy," I say, in a not particularly confident voice.

Ahead of me, Mr. Linsley urges his mare forward, and Blaze gives another unsettling lunge into a full gallop.

I rein him in. Oh heavens, we seem to be heading straight for a large tree. I duck to avoid its branches, then pull on the reins to turn the horse and assume some sort of control.

I have often wondered how it feels to fly, and for a very brief moment experience that exhilaration I have hitherto enjoyed only in dreams. The world blurs into a kaleidoscope of blue sky, green trees and grass, whirls, thumps the air from my lungs, and settles on Inigo's face.

I feel most peculiar—my head hurts and people's voices echo and bang inside my skull. And I am lying—no, I am reclining against something warm and strong and in my ear is a rhythmic thump. A heartbeat.

Inigo. Inigo's heart. Right next to me, against my cheek, and I don't want to move, even if I thought I could.

But what on earth has happened?

Julia leans over me. Tears run down her face. "Philomena, dearest, speak to us."

The arms around me clutch me tighter. "Philomena, for God's sake, tell me you are not hurt!"

I move my head to look into Inigo's face and what I see surprises me. He looks grim, older; and above all, he looks frightened.

"What's the matter?" So I still can speak, and now I remember flying off the horse—I hope my skirts stayed down—but if they did not, it is too late to worry about such a thing, and besides, I am too tired. "What are you doing, Inigo?"

"Holding you, my love. Are you hurt?"

"No. No, I don't think so. Bumped my head . . ." I move my arms and legs in a cautious sort of way. Yes, everything seems to be working, but I'm not inclined to move. My body is heavy and strange although my aching head seems to float.

"Brandy for the lady, sir." Someone thrusts a flask at us.

Inigo raises me slightly and the brandy stings my mouth and all the way down into my belly.

I consider the brandy, my floating head, and the oddness of my surroundings that, other than the strong warmth of Inigo, seem to move and shift in odd ways.

"Inigo?"

"Yes, my love?"

"I don't think the brandy was a very good idea." Inside me things are roiling in an unpleasant way and rather too slowly I realize what is happening. If I felt less strange and slow of wit I should be able to warn Inigo that I am about to vomit, which I do, and rather copiously, over my habit—only it is not mine, I borrowed it from Julia, and now it is ruined—and all over one of Inigo's beautifully polished boots.

Oh, this is dreadful. I squeeze my eyes tightly shut. I could not help it, but how shall I ever face him again?

"Philomena!" His voice is shocked. "Oh, sweetheart, I'm so sorry—"

Why should he be sorry? I threw up on him, after all.

"Out of the way, Inigo." Julia, her voice calm and kind, puts her arms around me and Inigo moves away from me. "Oh, Philomena, dearest, don't cry. It's not your fault."

When I consider it safe, I open my eyes. Julia hands me a handkerchief and we both try to smile at each other.

She leans forward. "I vomited all over Terrant once."

Well, that is a relief.

"In bed."

Oh, how dreadful.

"On our wedding night."

I am horrified.

"I think I ate too much at the wedding breakfast. He was very kind about it, although the Dowager Countess has never forgiven me for the damage to the bedcurtains—they were quite ruined. Terrant's great-great-great-grandmother embroidered them during the Spanish Armada, or while waiting to be beheaded, or some such."

As she speaks, she mops me up with our combined petticoats. It is not a very good job, but the best we can do. I am feeling a little better and the strange, echoing world recedes a little.

A footman, who looks somewhat familiar, pushes his way through the crowd. He bows to Lord Terrant, who stands to one side with Inigo. "My lord, Lady Rowbotham is here with her barouche, and will be pleased to take Miss Wellesley-Clegg home."

My aunt Rowbotham, peculiarly attired and dusted lightly with snuff, approaches. She glares at Terrant and shoves her pug Roland into his arms. Then she turns to Inigo. "Murderer!"

"Madam, I—"

"I always said you'd come to no good, Linsley." She bends, with a strange creaking sound—it must be her stays. "Philomena, my dear, let me take you from this wicked man and his horrible horse."

"It wasn't the horse's fault, Aunt. Or Mr. Linsley's."

My aunt makes a rude, snorting sound. "I daresay he's

only after your money. I'll take you home, my dear, and you need never see this villain again. Let me help you to my barouche."

In Terrant's arms the pug pants evilly, and leers at us with bulging black eyes.

Inigo pushes forward and to my surprise—and I must confess, to my delight—scoops me into his arms. I am afraid I must stink quite horribly and I am damp and rumpled, but I am very pleased to be there. And, of course, it gives me an excuse to put my arm around his neck. I am tremendously grateful that Julia gave me a violet pastille and I do not have to twist my head aside to avoid breathing horribly upon him.

He no longer looks frightened. Instead, he looks angry. His blue eyes blaze. "You silly little ninny, why didn't you say you couldn't ride? What do you think—"

I struggle to release myself from his arms. "I can ride, and don't call me names! I am not a ninny. You call me names far too often. It is most ungentlemanly."

He growls, "I thought you were dead. You almost killed *me*, you frightened me so badly! I think we should call off this absurd engagement immediately—"

"I beg your pardon, sir." It is difficult to brace oneself indignantly when the gentleman in question is holding you tightly against his chest and only your feet can express indignation with violent kicks. "It is the lady's prerogative to decide when the engagement ends."

Terrant steps forward. "Stubble it, Ratsarse."

I giggle. "*What* did you call him?"

Terrant smiles while Inigo scowls most horribly at him. "I called him Ratsarse, Miss Wellesley-Clegg. It's what we called him at school."

"Ratsarse!" How delightful!

Inigo mutters into my ear, "If you ever call me that, I swear I will spread a rumor at White's that you have spent all your capital on bonnets, swear abominably—"

"How very ungentlemanly of you!"

"And then," he hoists me closer against his chest and his breath tickles the top of my head—Julia follows behind with my hat—"no gentleman will ever marry you . . . Philly."

"You are a beast. I am not sorry I was sick over you."

Inigo adds in a casual manner that does not fool me for an instant, "And, by the way, my brother is called Pudgebum, and he would take it as a mark of extreme affability if you use that name to him."

"I think that is a dreadful lie. I am sure he would hate it. Anyone would."

He deposits me in my aunt's barouche and I rest my head against the leather squabs and close my eyes, afflicted with sudden weariness. "Will you . . . will you ride home with me?"

"Of course." He clears his throat. "Forgive me. I did not realize Blaze would be too much for you. I should have chosen you a more docile mount."

Well, it is time for me to confess. "You are right in thinking I do not ride, or barely. I ride a very sweet horse. She is called Strawberry and is twenty-three years old."

"Sweetheart . . ."

He has called me *sweetheart*? How charming—I believe he did so earlier when my head was quite addled—it would be even more charming if he meant it, or at least meant it half an hour hence. He sits next to me and wraps something warm and woollen around me. From the strong odor of pug, I deduce the shawl belongs to Roland.

"Promise me you will rest when you are at home." He tucks me in so I am cocooned like a silkworm, but I rather enjoy his attention. "I am afraid you will be rather bruised and stiff for a few days, after such a fall."

The barouche rocks and sways and more dog odor wafts our way. My aunt and Roland have arrived, both of them looking at Inigo with distaste, although I believe that is the pug's normal expression. I open my eyes so I may thank my aunt for her kindness.

"Pray do not take any notice of him, Philomena, whatever nonsense he may be telling you. Linsley, I see no reason for you to hold my niece's hand."

Why so he is, and neither of us is wearing gloves. I wish I felt better and could appreciate better his warm, firm hand wrapped around mine.

Inigo does not move. "I'm taking her pulse."

In answer to this bare-faced bit of insolence, Lady Rowbotham ignores us both for the rest of the journey.

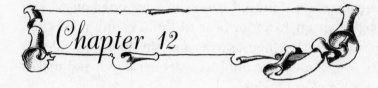

Chapter 12

Miss Philomena Wellesley-Clegg

Poor Inigo.

I have been sick on his boots, he has been insulted by his brother and my aunt Rowbotham, and now there is Mama.

"Oh Philly my dear my poor darling oh how could he do this to you why that habit will be ruined and his boots too but it serves him right sir you have acted monstrously towards my dear girl and I shall never forgive you never oh this engagement should never have taken place and I shall not blame her if she breaks it off in fact I think she should Hen where have you been all this while we must send for the physician and put poor Philly to bed Mr. Linsley if my poor girl does not last the night it shall weigh forever upon your conscience if indeed you even have one you wicked wicked man oh I cannot bear to think of my poor child married to such a one as you and she looks so pale oh Philly . . ." and so on, until Hen sits her down and makes her drink a glass of wine.

Inigo does not reply.

"I will not break off the engagement, Mama." I gather the damp and smelly skirts of the habit to go upstairs. "Hen, I wish to take a bath. Good-bye, Inigo."

"Philomena . . ." He takes my hand and kisses it. He looks quite wretched, and although I should like to reassure him, I am too tired and unwell to do more than squeeze his fingers in farewell before taking refuge in my room.

For the first time in my life I ask Mama to leave me alone, with Hen to look after me.

Mr. Inigo Linsley

I never thought I should agree with anything Mrs. Wellesley-Clegg says—for one thing, there is so much she says it is difficult to separate the wheat from the chaff. Imagine enough chaff to fill the dome of St. Paul's, for instance, and you have some idea of the dear lady's volubility. However, in this case she is right. I almost killed her darling, and this engagement was definitely a bad idea, although for different reasons than the ones she gave.

I may be able to replace a broken statue, but I cannot replace a broken child—something I am keenly aware of since Will came into the world. Shall I feel the same way, convinced my child is a fragile creature still, two decades in the future?

I skulk around the house for the rest of the day, aware my brother thinks me a fool—well, after my outburst I think I am a fool, too. Julia is quite kind to me, but then she usually is. Mama seems of a mind with Mrs. Wellesley-Clegg, and that damned Admiral visits us yet once again.

I do what any gentleman would do under the circumstances: get most horribly drunk. I really cannot remember much more of the evening.

As soon as decently possible the next day, and as soon as I can stand without feeling I shall cast my accounts, I take a dose of willow for the headache (in a small glass of brandy to aid the efficacy), and set off for the Wellesley-Cleggs' house. Halfway there I remember I cannot possibly arrive empty-handed, and halt the hackney to buy some flowers from a street vendor. I offer her a guinea for all the primroses she has—they grow wild everywhere at Weaselcopse at this time of year, and I like their scent and pale yellow—the color of the gown Philomena wore the day I first met her. I give the girl another five shillings for her basket, and thus laden, arrive at the house.

There is no straw, or muffled knocker, which is a good sign, and the footman does not look unduly sad when he admits me to the house. Neither Mrs. Wellesley-Clegg, Mr. Wellesley-Clegg, nor Miss Wellesley-Clegg is available, and since I did not expect to see Philomena downstairs at that hour of day, I do not take it amiss. All is well.

"Mr. Linsley?" The drawing-room door opens and the Weird Sisters stand there.

"Good morning, ladies."

They look at each other, and then at me. One of them clutches a book, and the other a drawing tablet.

"I have come to inquire after your sister's health," I say, in case they think me always encumbered by approximately twenty bunches of primroses.

"Will you not come in, Mr. Linsley?"

I hand my hat and gloves to the footman and enter the drawing room. I feel as though I am entering an enchanted cave, and when I leave, I will find a couple of centuries have passed and people travel by flying machines or some such.

The two creatures stare unblinking at me. They are tall and gangly, with none of Philomena's prettiness, but a certain foxy appeal in their narrow faces.

I balance the basket of flowers on the sofa beside me. "I trust I find you in good health, Miss Lydia, Miss Charlotte. And which of you is which today?"

"I am Charlotte," says the one with a pink ribbon.

"Is it true you have a baby, Mr. Linsley?" says Lydia, who may well be Charlotte.

Good God. "Yes, I do."

"But you are not married."

I am not prepared to give these ethereal creatures an education of that sort. "How is your sister?"

They glance at each other with extreme gravity.

"She is in bed upstairs."

The one with the drawing tablet hands a sheet of paper to me.

She has made a fairly competent pencil sketch. It shows a woman in bed, her hair loose, eyes closed, hands crossed over her breast.

A young and beautiful woman.

Philomena.

For one dreadful moment I forget how to breathe. The paper rattles in my hand.

Philomena.

Then I leap to my feet, knocking the flowers over, and blunder out of the room, round the corner to the staircase, bashing my knee on the plinth where the unfortunate Hebe once stood, and up the stairs.

The first room I stumble into is deserted, save for a maid who is making the bed and looks up, her mouth opening in fear; I must indeed look like a madman. I run to the next door, push it open with such violence it bounces off the wall, and stop dead.

Philomena, sitting up in bed, screams.

I can hardly blame her. "I thought—I thought—" I can barely speak. I hold the paper out to her, my hand shaking like a leaf.

She clutches a pillow to herself.

I drop onto a corner of the bed, clasping the bedpost, my chest heaving as though I have just run a mile. It's abominably rude, but I cannot wait for her to ask me to sit. "Your—your sister. Don't know which one. Gave me—gave me—this. I thought—"

Footsteps pound up the stairs. A man, the footman from downstairs, speaks. "Are you all right, Miss Wellesley-Clegg?"

"Yes, thank you, Simon." To me she hisses, "What are you *doing* here?"

My knee, which I injured on my flight upstairs, begins to throb. "I thought you were dead."

Very slowly, she uncurls from her pillow and reaches out to snatch the paper in her fingertips, like a stray dog accepting food. She looks at it, and then at me. "I offered to pose for Lydia."

"So I see."

Now I am sure my legs will hold me, I stand and bow. As I do so, I notice for the first time the condition of the invalid's bedchamber. A novel, face down, lies on the bed, along with the latest copy of the *Lady's Magazine*, some sort of dress-making project, and a large bowl of sweetmeats. And Philomena herself, wearing a very pretty nightrail, from what I can see of it behind the pillow, with her small, delicate feet curved on the bed. I notice what lovely toes she has.

And she's alive. Thank God. I shall definitely go to church more often.

I lunge for the sweetmeats. I cannot, after all, lunge for her. "I haven't had breakfast," I explain.

"Oh, very well."

"I didn't mean to frighten you," I say through a mouthful of Turkish delight. "I'm sorry. How do you feel today?"

"I'm much better," she says in a small voice. "Mama thought I should stay in bed."

"What are you reading?"

"Nothing."

She grabs the book before I can reach it. It is what Julia always does when I catch her reading something frivolous, so I think it best not to pursue the question.

She looks at the drawing again, frowns, and bellows in a voice I did not know she possessed, "Lydia!"

We hear someone come up the stairs, and a twin pokes her head around the door.

"Send your sister!" Philomena roars.

The girl disappears, and shortly after, the other, I presume, for Philomena does not send her away, enters the room.

"You are to apologize immediately to Mr. Linsley, Lydia."

Lydia gazes at her feet. "I am sorry, Mr. Linsley."

"There is no harm done, Miss Lydia."

"Fortunately not." Philomena rips the drawing into pieces. "What if you had showed that to our aunt Rowbotham? It could well have killed her, you silly, foolish girl. Now go away. And, no, you may not have a sweetmeat."

Lydia curtsies and leaves the room. When I turn back to Philomena, she has taken advantage of the second or so I took to open the door for her sister to swathe herself in a large shawl.

"I am not used to gentlemen invading my bedchamber."

"I should hope not." We stare at each other. It is damnably awkward.

"You were right," she says after a while. "I ache all over. I have some horrible bruises."

"Arnica helps."

"Yes. I am sorry about your boot. Is it ruined?"

"It looks rather unusual. Maybe I could get someone to puke over the other one so they match again."

Our uninspired conversation is interrupted by the entry of Hen, two footmen, the maid, and the twins, carrying vases and bowls full of primroses. They place them around the room, careful not to notice my presence, for of course a virtuous young lady could not possibly receive a gentleman, even one to whom she is betrothed, in her bedchamber.

"I'll send up some tea, miss," Hen says. "And Mr. and Mrs. Wellesley-Clegg will be back from church soon." This is said with a warning glance in my direction.

Church? Oh, good God, it is Sunday, and I have broken a vow already, although I suppose I could go to Evensong. It certainly explains why there were so few street vendors around.

Hen leaves the room, singing. I catch a few words, something about sinners, eternal fire, and salvation, and wonder whether it is a discreet warning to me.

"The flowers are lovely."

Philomena looks transformed. She holds a bowl of them on her lap, and her smile almost makes my knees buckle again.

"Good. I'm afraid I dropped them downstairs when I thought . . . they remind me of you. Little and sweet and delicate . . ." I sound like a fool.

"They remind me of home."

"Me too."

"I've never been given flowers before, and there are so many of them."

Almost every horizontal surface of the room, mantelpiece,

dressing-table, and table, are covered with primroses. Their scent fills the air, wild and sweet.

Like her.

She slithers off the bed and walks over to me. "Thank you, Inigo."

And then she kisses me.

Chapter 13

Miss Philomena Wellesley-Clegg

I cannot believe how brazen I have become.

I had wondered about kissing, how you got your faces in the right place and do not merely bump noses. Inigo seems quite good at it, but I believe he has had some practice.

So I put my lips against his, my head tilted a little to one side—I have put some thought into this. I have put a lot of thought into it, I am afraid to say. I have told myself I should learn to kiss a man in case my future husband requires it of me, but the sad fact is that I want to kiss Inigo, not some faceless stranger.

He tenses for just a moment and makes no move to draw

closer to me—I am not pressed lewdly against him although I think I should like to be. So only our mouths touch, and my hands rest on his shoulder. It is quite friendly and gentle, as our lips move, slowly nibbling and pressing.

His hands move to cup my face, and now I am pressed against him, and it is wicked. I might as well be unclothed.

So I am a wanton. I slide my tongue against his lips and he hesitates and parts his lips. I am kissing him, there is no doubt about it, I lead and he follows.

"I think we'd best stop this," he says and lets me go.

He walks away from me and stares out of the window, his back to me, and I can see something is wrong.

Oh, I am such a fool.

"It's not your fault," he says, as though he knows how confused and embarrassed I now am.

I wrap myself in the shawl and sit on the edge of the bed. "I'm sorry."

"Philomena, it's . . ." He's talking with his back to me, which is rather rude, and his voice is tight. "You don't know very much about men."

"Of course I don't! I was rather hoping you might teach me."

"Nothing would give me greater pleasure, but you know I can't. Your husband will expect you to learn from him. I'm only human, my love. I'm alone in a bedchamber with you, you're barely clothed, and . . . Well, you remember how it was when Blaze took it into his mind to gallop?"

"Oh, indeed yes."

"It's like that for a man, Philomena."

"Is this something to do with Needs?"

"Well, yes. If I were a horse at this moment I would want

to gallop off and fling myself over hedges, until . . . Good God, Philomena, surely you see what I mean."

"I think so." I feel that way a little myself. "Blaze reminded me of you. He was so very muscular and unpredictable."

"I really don't think we should be alone together." His head is bowed. He picks at a flake of loose paint on the windowsill with his thumbnail.

"You're probably right."

"My love, the offer stands to end this farce. Anytime you wish."

He has called me his love, and I know it is from kindness, and because he does care for me in his way. I saw that when he thought I was dead, both times. He would have mourned me, I am sure, and maybe kept my memory in a corner of his heart. But I do not think it would have been much more, or for very long.

"Philomena, don't cry." He sits beside me and hands over his handkerchief.

"If—if I break the engagement Julia will hate me. My family will be so disappointed. If I tell them I have deceived them, it will be even worse."

"Blame it on me," he says.

"I can't do that!"

"You may as well. My family will do so, however it ends."

"How else could it end?" I ask, but Inigo springs to his feet and steps away as we hear someone coming up the stairs.

It is Hen, with tea, but only for me. It is as though Inigo is invisible.

"You need to rest, miss. You look all shaken up again." She

bundles me back into bed and straightens out the sheets as though erasing the traces of a wild romp.

"I hope you feel better soon, Miss Wellesley-Clegg."

How I wish he could kiss my hand, but Hen is planted in the way.

"Good-bye. Thank you for the flowers."

He bows, and I am glad Hen does not say a word.

I plan to be asleep when Mama and Papa return. What is the harm of one more small deception?

Chapter 14

Miss Philomena Wellesley-Clegg

The next day I am recovered enough to pay afternoon calls, and naturally we visit the Terrants so Mama and the Dowager Countess can gossip. Julia, it appears, is resting, but will be downstairs shortly, so I find myself talking to Admiral Sev, a most pleasant gentleman.

He looks across the room at the Dowager Countess and shakes his head, smiling. "Aye, a fine figure of a woman, is she not? And it's good to see her laugh." He glances at the portrait on the wall. "Still d—d handsome, beg your pardon, Miss Philomena—she was considered a great beauty in her prime. I'd like to have had her likeness as a figurehead for a ship."

I imagine the Dowager Countess, eyes wide above the foam, frightening off the French, and agree she would be most effective.

"I wonder," he continues, "strictly between you and me, Miss Philomena, why she hasn't married again. Do you think—"

"Sev!" The Dowager Countess summons him and he leaps to his feet. "I have need of your nimble fingers."

"She likes me to sort out her embroidery silks," he explains. "I have some dexterity from tying knots all these years." He bows and ambles across the room to her side, where he busies himself with a mess of colored silks. It is a most peaceful and happy scene, the Dowager Countess smiling upon him occasionally, while she and Mama cackle and gossip.

I should like to talk to Julia about Sev and the Dowager Countess, but every time I try to raise the subject, she changes it, and Mr. Linsley seems quite oblivious of what is under his nose. As for Terrant, I think he would not be well pleased that a mere second cousin, and a commoner, courts their mama.

The door opens, but it is only Julia, who smiles at me—in truth, I was quite unaware of how excited I must look to see the door open, and I feel foolish.

"It is so charming to see my best friend and my favorite brother-in-law so deeply in love," she comments. "I have lectured Inigo most severely on allowing you to ride Blaze, and he is quite contrite. But tell me, Philomena, will you announce the engagement at your ball? It is not fair to keep every eligible bachelor on tenterhooks indefinitely."

I am excessively relieved that the door opens at that moment to admit Miss Celia Blundell, who eyes the cakes and biscuits greedily.

I ask Celia and Julia if she knows of anyone who has a maid looking for a new position. I have come to the conclusion that Hen, as much as I shall miss her, is right—it is too much work for her, and she will not want to leave Mama.

Julia says not. She seems distracted. Then she bursts out, "Ladies, I know this is not a committee meeting, but I am most concerned about our Association. All we do is talk and talk, our benefit concert by dear Amelia has raised barely enough money to print a pamphlet as we planned, and how we are ever going to afford anything else seems impossible. I am quite in despair."

Julia looks so unhappy, I cast about for something to cheer her up.

A scent of horse, and dare I say it, a familiar male smell becomes evident.

I will not look round. I know he is somewhere behind me.

I hear the creak of leather, and a rustle of fabric, and know that Inigo stands beside my chair. His arm reaches out for the dwindling supply of refreshments, and somehow, as he does so, his other hand tickles my neck.

"Good afternoon, ladies."

"What do you want, Inigo?" Julia sounds very cross. This is so unlike her, for she is naturally of a sunny disposition, that I am quite concerned.

"I believe I have the answer to your dilemma."

Miss Blundell mumbles something around a mouthful, and Julia snorts.

"Seriously, ladies, here's the catch. Your Association has not yet proved its worth. It exists in name only. You need rescue only one fallen woman and show that she can become a useful member of society, and your case will be made. Donations will flood in, and the Strand will be transformed."

"That's all very well, Inigo, but we cannot go searching out a fallen woman and have nothing for her to do."

"Miss Wellesley-Clegg." He winks at me. "You have a need for a maid, I believe."

"Well, yes, but I . . ." Now he is in my view I become the hopeless dithering creature I usually am around him. He has been riding—hence the scent of horse—and wears buff buckskins, very tight, but I look only once and glance away, then back to make sure I did see what I thought, and, oh . . . it is hopeless.

"Many lightskirts—or so I believe—enter the profession after they lost jobs in service, or as seamstresses," Inigo says. He sounds quite knowledgeable.

"Why, that gives me an idea," Julia says. "Philomena, if we find one, Hen could train her, and then she could be your maid when you are married."

"How do you know so much about fallen women, Mr. Linsley?"

He stares at me and drops his whip.

I shall not watch him bend to pick it up.

Only a little.

Oh.

"Philomena!"

"Yes, Julia?"

"Will you second the motion?"

"Oh, yes. Certainly. Should I write it down?" What motion?

Miss Blundell makes a mumbling sound with her mouth full.

"Thank you. The motion was seconded by Miss Celia Blundell."

"Good."

Inigo sits in a chair opposite me and I look away. I really must not stare at him. Celia Blundell is the biggest gossip I know, other than myself, Julia, and my sister.

"Exactly how do you mean to go about this, Julia, my dear?" Inigo asks.

"Why, you shall escort us to a house of ill fame and select a woman for us to interview," Julia replies.

Mr. Inigo Linsley

I don't like this at all.

Now Philomena believes I am a great whoremonger, in addition to my other faults.

"I didn't second the motion," Miss Blundell says. "I asked what we should wear."

"Oh, of course."

The three of them enter into an animated conversation on the sartorial aspects of such an expedition.

My dear little Philomena has a refurbished dress and a new bonnet she very much wants to show off.

Julia thinks they should dress plainly, like nuns or Quakers.

Miss Blundell says something unintelligible which the other two consider and discuss with some gravity regarding new sleeves.

I interrupt them. "Ladies, since we attend in the evening, you should dress as for the opera, with hooded cloaks, and you might also want to consider masks in case any gentlemen of your acquaintance are present."

"I am sure we do not know anyone who frequents such places," Julia says with a sniff.

I agree, hoping that old, bad habits do not send my brother seeking diversions after an arduous late session in the House, and suggest the enterprise should take place the next evening.

Again, there is much discussion. It is a good thing women do not have the vote, for they would not be satisfied until all agree, a most dreadful form of government. Tonight, Monday, is apparently out of the question; there is some event that all three ladies are determined to attend. Tuesday, tomorrow, is debated with great gravity and little substance. Wednesday, of course, is Almack's, and that is sacred.

Another long, rambling conversation takes place on how we are to get there. Terrant may need his carriage, and we certainly don't want the gossipmongers of the town talking of how it was seen outside Mrs. Bright's establishment. The three ladies agree with me that they should meet here, and then we shall take a hackney.

It is an exhausting process. If I did not have Philomena to watch I think I should go mad, or fall asleep.

"Miss Wellesley-Clegg," I say finally when they seem to be crawling to a consensus, "I found that book in which you expressed an interest."

"The book—oh, *that* book." Bless her, she is incapable of guile.

"Yes, indeed. That book." We nod and smile at each other like a pair of imbeciles for a few minutes.

"That book. To be sure." She stands, knocking the plate of cakes from the footman's hand into Miss Blundell's lap, and a better destination for them I couldn't imagine.

I draw her aside.

"I trust you will not try to kiss me."

I try not to grin. She is enchanting when she puts on airs. "Only if you want me to, my dear."

I take a quick look around. At the far end of the drawing room, our dear mamas clasp each other's hands, lost in their girlhood recollections. Miss Blundell is eating—what else—and Julia is purposefully looking away.

"You are so arrogant."

"No, I'm not."

"You are."

"No, I—listen, you divine idiot, I wanted to tell you the deed was signed this morning, and Weaselcopse Manor is mine."

"Oh, Inigo." She clasps my hands in hers. "I am so happy for you."

"Thank you." I feel an odd pang. She should not be this happy about something which originally hurt her feelings. "Philomena, will you accompany me and Julia tomorrow morning to buy a new statue for your papa?"

She beams at me. "Oh, certainly. I love to buy things."

"Excellent. I need to take care of that before I go down to Weaselcopse and make sure all is well there. I'll be away for a week or so."

"Oh, please come back in time for my coming-out ball. It is a se'ennight Saturday."

"I wouldn't miss it for the world." Why this should make me feel so uncomfortable, I have no idea.

"Oh, yes, I am sure I shall have an excellent choice of suitors there." She bites her lip and looks down.

I'd like to bite that perfect red lip, too.

"Inigo?" Her eyes are wonderful, gray and green with a rim of gold around the center. "How I wish you would marry."

"Maybe I will, now I have my own house and land."

"Oh, yes, you should."

This is unbearable, her suffocating kindness. We both know her prettiness and fortune will find her a husband with little difficulty, and the idea does not sit well with me. I am a younger son of bad reputation whose duty is to marry as well as I can, and indeed, I have few choices.

My inclination is to marry a small, rounded woman with curly hair and multi-colored eyes who kisses like an angel.

I doubt I shall.

Chapter 15

Mr. Inigo Linsley

Julia looks a fright the next morning at breakfast.

"I'm breeding," she snaps at me, and then clutches my sleeve. "Don't tell Terrant, for if you do he may stay home tonight, and I would not miss it for the world."

"Yes, but . . . do you think it such an outing wise under the circumstances?" I remember Fanny in a similar condition, alternately raging, and falling asleep at odd times, and prone to all sorts of odd fancies. "And while I'm most honored you should confide in me, surely you should tell my brother?"

"Oh, *him*," she snarls, and shoves a slice of toast into her mouth as though she had been taking lessons from Miss Blundell.

I do not pursue the matter further.

Philomena arrives, looking delectable as usual, and she and Julia embark on a long discussion of gowns, trims, and bonnets, from which I gather her gown was a former lost cause but somehow the acquisition of the bonnet made all well. I try to look interested and intelligent, wondering if this is how women feel when men discuss politics or horses.

"I must fetch my book," Julia says, with a meaningful look at me. "I shall be back shortly."

"Oh, Inigo." Philomena clasps my hands as Julia leaves the room. "I had such a fine time last night. I had hoped you might be there—it was Lady Frostingham's ball—but I received much attention from gentlemen."

"Good." The word forces itself out of me.

"Tell me, what do you know of a Mr. Danbury? And Lord Charisbrooke? And the Viscount Effingford, who was most persistent?"

I grit my teeth. It occurs to me that I could ruin Philomena's hopes by telling an outrageous lie, that all three of her prospective suitors are diseased reprobates with a dozen bastards and in debt up to their ears. I'm tempted to do it before my better feelings come to the fore.

"Danbury has a moderate fortune; he's not clever, but a good enough fellow. Charisbrooke gambles too much, but I think it from boredom. Effingford needs to marry money, and soon, for his estate is in a sorry way . . . But Philomena, which of them do you like?"

"I like them all well enough, but none of them as much—"

Julia comes back into the drawing room before Philomena can make me rage with jealousy even more. "Well, come along, Inigo," she says to me, as if it is I who keep them waiting.

Miss Philomena Wellesley-Clegg

We set off in Terrant's carriage. Inigo seems somewhat out of sorts; Julia too.

I wonder what he would have done if I had said what was on my mind, that I liked him better than the gentlemen I met last night? Would he have laughed? I don't believe so, for I know him to be a kind gentleman; why, he is even kind to his mother, who despite Captain Sev's influence and her friendship with Mama, is still a frightening sort of woman. More likely he would have been sorry for me and I don't think I could bear that.

Apparently I am the one to make conversation. "What did you do last night, Inigo?"

Julia glares at him.

"I visit Will on Monday nights."

"How is he?"

"In great spirits. I shall have to get him a cricket ball soon, for he delights in throwing things. His first tooth has come through, and he drools mightily."

"You don't give babies cricket balls," Julia says in disgust. I suspect this is family code for *You do not talk of your b—d in polite company.*

"Where is it exactly we are going, Inigo?" I ask.

"To Mr. Totterton's Emporium of Antiquities. I'm sure he'll have a statue Mr. Wellesley-Clegg will like. How are your papa and mama?"

"In rather low spirits, I am afraid. My brother Robert wrote that the chimneypiece in the morning room has a crack some three inches wide." I look out of the window and recognize the streets. We are very close to Fanny's house. "Oh, is this not near where—"

Before Inigo can answer, Julia intervenes. "I am feeling rather fatigued this morning, so I shall read while you view Mr. Totterton's goods."

In other words, she is kind enough to offer us a tête-à-tête in which I shall try not to think about Inigo kissing me, or me kissing him.

Opposite me, Inigo sighs gustily. To me it does not sound like a sigh of anticipation.

Inigo hands Julia and me down at Mr. Totterton's establishment, and holds the shop door open for us to enter.

The building is old and has a dusty smell and uneven floors. The first thing I see is a stuffed crocodile hanging from the ceiling.

"Splendid, is it not?" Inigo says. "I tried to buy it once for Will, but Fanny objected so violently I did not pursue the matter. It is just the sort of thing I should have liked as my own when I was a boy."

"Oh, this is a wonderful place, indeed, Inigo." I'm glad to see he has cheered up a little, even if it is only to talk about his mistress.

Mr. Totterton, a portly, courteous gentleman, brings Julia tea and a comfortable chair, and Inigo and I make our way into the depths of the shop. I do not know what the building was before Mr. Totterton moved in, perhaps some sort of warehouse, for it is a maze of crooked rooms opening one from the other, with uneven floors.

Mr. Totterton accompanies us. "Statues, sir? Why, of course I have statues, suitable for every taste, Mr. Linsley. A most elegant Cupid in the third room to the right, and a likeness of Alexander the Great in bronze in the room beyond that, are in new. But look around, sir."

There seems to be no known logic to Mr. Totterton's arrangement. All sorts of things, furniture, ornaments, china, and silver, are piled haphazardly in each room.

"Oh, look, Inigo. Can that be a carved dragon? How did you find this place?"

"Fanny and I bought a bed here." He looks away. "I beg your pardon. That was most indelicate."

"Why? You had to sleep on something." I suppose it is not the allusion to sleep that embarrasses him. Nevertheless I walk away quickly into the next room, where I find a statue, and stand quite still in front of it, taken aback by its beauty.

Mr. Inigo Linsley

The statue is not one her papa would appreciate, for it is a copy of Michelangelo's *David*. Her back is turned to me, but I hear her breath quicken. Then she reaches out her hand, which is bare—I did not see her remove her glove—and touches the statue's shoulder. Her fingers trail down the creamy marble, down to David's flank.

Good God. It is as though I feel that touch on my own skin. She turns to me, and I see a look in her eyes I have seen on only a few women (not counting the ones who have been paid to assume such an expression)—naked desire.

My breathing comes fast now, and to my embarrassment I am highly aroused, and she cannot help but notice.

There's confusion in her gaze, too—an innocent young woman such as she cannot understand what she feels.

If my mouth had not gone suddenly dry, I should jest about how my head is certainly bigger in proportion to my body, but unfortunately at the moment I have other attributes greater than David's, and my brain clouds over.

"Inigo?"

"Ah, yes, a very fine copy," I blabber, and turn to take refuge behind a tall chest of drawers. In so doing, I misjudge my distended anatomy and sweep a handful of china ornaments off a table and onto the floor.

"Dear, dear, that will be thirteen shillings and sixpence, Mr. Linsley." Mr. Totterton has arrived to keep an eye on his stock.

Aware that I am being grossly overcharged—doubtless Mr. Totterton has levied a breakage by arousal surcharge on the price—I arrive safely behind the chest of drawers. "Indeed, add it to the bill, if you please."

Mr. Totterton bows and returns to the front of his shop, doubtless glad to have rid himself of items that, from the dust on the table, must have been there for some time.

I force myself to think about blood, ice, and dead dogs.

Philomena now looks only confused, until her face disappears behind the brim of her bonnet as she turns away to continue her search.

When I am fit to be seen again I emerge from my hiding-place and go in search of her. She will not meet my eyes.

"Look, Inigo, do you not think this quite the thing?" She indicates the statue of a shepherdess, not a nipple in sight.

"Yes, it's quite elegant, but I think your papa had something more classical in mind."

"Of course."

My attention is caught by a nymph lurking between a stuffed owl leaking sawdust, and a large china vase. She has a vapid smile and is too silly to cover herself with the copious drapery that cascades around her feet. An impractical-looking bow is carved to hang from one shoulder, and something, I think it a sort of dog, lounges beside her.

"How about this, Philomena?"

She looks at it, her head tilted to one side. "I don't know. It is very . . ."

Very naked. *Dead dog frozen in a patch of ice.*

"A most pleasing example of the classical style. Note the artistry of the, ah, the drapery. The perfection of the female form presented in an entirely tasteful fashion." *Buckets of blood.* "I think your papa and mama would both find it extremely correct."

"Oh, do you think so?" She is not entirely convinced, I can tell.

Mr. Totterton appears, smirking at me in a man-to-man fashion. "You will find Mr. Linsley's taste impeccable, miss. He has bought some most excellent, if old-fashioned, pieces here."

To my ears it sounds obscene and I wonder if he is about to reminisce about the beauties of the bed, the very large bed, Fanny and I bought here.

Philomena smiles at him. "Whom does this represent, Mr. Totterton?"

"Why, Diana, miss, the virgin goddess of the hunt. Such fine marble, too. A beautiful piece. I must admit I am reluctant to part with her."

"My sister's name is Diana. Are you sure Papa will like this, Inigo?"

"Only twenty guineas, Mr. Linsley."

I take him aside, not wanting Philomena to hear vulgar bickerings about payment. "Ten, Mr. Totterton. There is a large crack on its arse."

"It is an antique, sir! Why, that probably happened when the Goths invaded Rome, or some such. Eighteen."

"More like when your assistant dropped it off the cart. Twelve."

"I trust the bed remains satisfactory, sir? Seventeen."

"Only if you include the broken china in that price, Mr. Totterton. Thirteen."

He sighs tremulously and blows his nose on a large, stained handkerchief. "Sixteen, sir, and I dare not go lower."

"Very well. Sixteen." We shake hands, and Mr. Totterton beams with pleasure in a way that makes me think he has made a very good bargain indeed, although the bed, to give him his due, has seen excellent service.

More dead dogs.

Miss Philomena Wellesley-Clegg

I do not know what came over me at Mr. Totterton's establishment. I quite blush to think of it now, for it was most awkward.

The statue was so beautiful, so very smooth and creamy. As I touched it I could not help but think of how a real man might feel. I willed my fingers to translate cool marble into warm flesh, and I am afraid I thought specifically of Inigo, whose body is the only male one I have felt pressed close to me. Fully clothed, of course. Hot, shivery, indecent feelings filled me and I could scarcely breathe.

I heard him draw breath sharply behind me and turned to see him staring at me. I should have been highly embarrassed to be caught touching a nude male (even if it was only a statue), and I admit a trace of decency remained in me, but it was over-ridden by other feelings which frightened and exhilarated me.

I am not so innocent that I could not observe (although to do so I had to look at that region I keep swearing I will look at no more, but somehow cannot seem to do so) his arousal.

Thank God the crash of breaking porcelain brought me to my senses, and blushing horribly, I escaped to collect my senses.

We barely spoke thereafter. Indeed, much of our earlier ease with each other has gone, and I feel unaccountably sad. It is high time I found a real suitor.

Julia, who seemed out of sorts, yawned all the way to our house and declined to come in for refreshment. She said we both needed to keep our wits about us for this evening. I wonder . . . they have been married some six months, but of course she will tell no one before Terrant, and that is quite right.

Oh, this evening will be so exciting! At last, the Association shall show fruit for its labors, and I shall see Inigo in his evening breeches, which are even tighter than his trousers.

I resolve I shall put aside a sixpence for the Association every time I think indecent thoughts. The episode today in Mr. Totterton's shop has raised at least two shillings and sixpence.

Chapter 16

Miss Philomena Wellesley-Clegg

After much reflection I choose the pink with blue trim for the evening's expedition, for it has been very much admired and shows off my bosom to great advantage. Not that I wish to tonight, of course, for I am sure no gentleman with whom I would wish to associate will be at Mrs. Bright's house. I must admit I am curious about such things. There are so many diversions gentlemen practice—both innocent, like cricket, or useful, like politics, or wicked, like gambling and consorting with w——s (again, were I a gentleman I should be allowed to spell out that word). We ladies, with our music, embroidery, archery, bonnets, *et cetera*, lead tame lives indeed by comparison.

And I wonder who made the rule that a woman like Mrs. Gibbons, a perfectly pleasant and hardworking person, is considered an object of depravity? As much as I like Fanny, I do not want to think that she and Inigo are possibly still lovers, or how that makes me feel—sad and jealous all at once.

I really must be pleasant to gentlemen tomorrow night at Almack's. Oh, surely there must be one who has Inigo's handsome features and kindness, and an equally interesting—

I write an IOU for my collection of sixpences, for I have only a guinea left and no change. I regret the fund is growing rather too fast.

After dinner Inigo, Julia, and Celia come to collect me in a hackney. Inigo seems somewhat distracted and stares out of the window. He is indeed wearing his dark blue breeches, and I tie a knot in the corner of my handkerchief to remind myself to add yet another sixpence to the collection.

The carriage pulls up outside a house in Grosvenor Square. I am confused. This is a most respectable area, and we have visited other houses here.

Inigo smiles as though reading my mind. "Do not concern yourself, Miss Wellesley-Clegg. I should not take you to an unfashionable place."

I attempt a toss of the head, which dislodges the headdress I made with some of the bright blue feathers from my new bonnet. I wish now I had not done so, for it will be tedious to retrim it.

As I straighten out the headdress, Inigo hands each of us a plain black mask. "Just in case," he says.

D—n! Does this mean I shall not be able to wear this dress in society again? I reassure myself that gentlemen never notice such things, and besides, it is only morally depraved wretches who frequent such places.

A footman in very ornate livery shows us into a most elegant drawing-room, with expensive carpets and wallpaper (coming from Trade I do notice such things), and the first person I see is the Bishop of W—! I am quite shocked for he has a wife, but perhaps he is here on a mission similar to ours.

"Linsley," he says. "I have not seen you here in a while. How's the fascinating Mrs. Gibbons?"

"As fascinating as ever," Inigo says.

I am shocked. So Inigo has been here before!

The Bishop nods and sits on a couch. To my astonishment, a woman young enough to be his daughter and very ladylike in appearance, wanders over and sits on his knee. Any hopes I had of the Bishop being here for virtuous reasons flee when he puts his face against her neck and makes loud smacking noises with his mouth.

"Good evening, Mr. Linsley." A middle-aged woman, also of a most respectable appearance and wearing an exceedingly elegant gown, approaches us. "How pleasant to see you again. Ladies, welcome."

He bows and kisses her hand. "You look as ravishing as always, Mrs. Bright."

"Oh, fie. You are an incorrigible flirt. And what do you have in mind this evening? But first, you will all take some wine, I trust?"

She nods at a footman, who fetches a bottle and some glasses, and we all sit.

I try not to watch the Bishop, who has now tugged up the woman's skirts, one meaty hand resting on her knee. She giggles and squirms on his lap.

Inigo and Mrs. Bright chat away together about the play and various mutual acquaintances, for all the world as though he pays an afternoon call. There are several gentlemen, and a dozen or so young ladies in the room, mostly behaving in a polite fashion. It could be a private party of the *ton*, except the ladies are a little more forward in conversation and gesture.

"Lord, I declare, that is the Duke of C—!" Celia whispers in my ear as a man, accompanied by another young woman, crosses the room in front of us.

"Why, so it is!" I have not been this close to a member of the royal family since my presentation at court, where no one's shirttails hung out in such a depraved fashion. The duke appears to be the worse for drink, and he has one hand thrust down the poor young woman's bosom. They both laugh heartily.

Mrs. Bright looks slightly distressed, as a hostess might if one of her guests spilled tea on the carpet. "I should like to introduce you to a new lady who has joined my household, Mr. Linsley. I am sure you and your companions will find her very pleasing."

"That's most kind, Mrs. Bright. But tell me, what was this young lady's former profession? Was she by any chance a seamstress?"

"I believe she may have been." She gives him a wicked look that would have cost me at least half a crown's worth of sixpences. "Are you having some trouble with your buttons, sir?"

Inigo laughs and kisses her hand.

Mrs. Bright nods to a woman at the far side of the room, who crosses to us and curtsies. I see a difference now. If a lady were to be introduced to a gentleman in polite society, he would of course stand and bow to her, but Inigo remains seated. As she curtsies, she leans forward so Inigo can look down her bosom, and I am afraid to say he does so.

"Ah, yes. I'm pleased to make your acquaintance, Miss . . . ?"

"My name is Kate, sir."

She is about my age, with fair hair and an ivory gown which is most elegant but cut so low as to make mine look almost decent. She casts a curious glance at us three ladies, then lowers her eyes in a demure manner.

"Raise your gown, my dear, so the gentleman can see your charms," Mrs. Bright murmurs.

"No, that won't be necessary, thank you!" Julia says.

"I assure you, miss, it's no trouble," Kate replies, one hand already hoisting her skirts. She looks at Inigo for direction.

"No need, Miss Kate," Inigo says.

"Indeed, maybe you would all care to adjoin to a private room?" Mrs. Bright is once again the elegant hostess. "Some more wine, and other refreshments? We have excellent oysters and lobster."

"A capital idea," Celia says. "I love lobster."

"Of course. Ladies, if you will excuse us, Mrs. Bright and I should discuss terms." Inigo and Mrs. Bright rise and move a few steps away.

It reminds me of Mr. Totterton's, when he and Inigo discussed a price for the statue and china. Snippets of conversation drift over to us.

"Why, sir, it is a fair enough price . . . but what you do there is no concern of mine . . . I cannot have any young ladies be tired by the attentions of more than one, so I must . . ."

"What on earth does she think we shall do?" Celia says.

"I assure you, Mrs. Bright, Kate will be as fresh as a daisy after an hour in our company," Inigo says.

She taps him on the shoulder with her fan. "Oh, so they all say, but I know what men are, sir, and women too . . . you forget, there is wear and tear on the bed to be considered also. Why, that bed is of the finest quality, as are all the furnishings in my house, but it is not built for five."

"Terrant will kill me and Inigo both if he ever hears of this," Julia whispers.

Inigo and Mrs. Bright's heads are close together, and I see him give her a handful of coins—several dozen guineas, from the look of it.

Kate, meanwhile, gives us a pleasant smile and sips from a glass of wine. She does not seem at all concerned that it is her person that is bartered.

After a few minutes more of whispered conversation, Mrs. Bright nods at Kate and summons a footman.

"This way, if you please, ladies, and sir," Kate says, and leads us out of the drawing room and up the stairs. She lifts her skirt, revealing most of her calves and ankles as we ascend the stairs, and she shows us into an elegant bedchamber.

As well as the bed, there are a sofa and several chairs, and we sit. Kate saunters to the bed and sits there, her feet swinging.

The footman enters with a small black boy who carries a folding table, and a cold collation of lobster and oysters is set out, along with more wine. It looks quite delicious, and I wish I had not eaten so much dinner. Celia, however, starts in on the lobster.

"Well, then, shall we commence?" Kate says. She stands and backs up to Inigo, looking over her shoulder at him.

He raises his hands as if to unhook her gown.

"Inigo!" Julia snaps.

"I beg your pardon." He looks embarrassed. "Ah, ladies, if you will excuse me . . . I shall be back shortly." Muttering something about credit, he leaves the room.

Julia, Celia and I look at each other.

"Let us give the gentleman a lovely surprise on his return," Kate says, and takes off her gown.

She is stark naked except for her stockings.

"Oh." I gulp. "What pretty garters."

Mr. Inigo Linsley

Of all the embarrassing things a gentleman has to do, establishing a line of credit at a nunnery, even one such as Mrs. Bright's establishment, must be the worst.

I brought as much cash with me as I could lay my hands on, but it is not enough. I know the refreshments will be priced astronomically high, but hoped that Mrs. Bright would allow a special price for merely talking to one of her girls. She does not believe that for a moment, and neither does she believe the ladies I brought with me will be only observers.

"Well, sir," she says finally with a charming, yet steely smile, "you must see the captain."

"The captain, madam?"

"Yes, indeed. He sees to my business arrangements. You will find him upstairs."

I have no choice. Hoping only that Miss Blundell will not order more food in my absence, I ask a footman to direct me to the captain who keeps the ship of pleasure afloat.

The first thing I see upon entering the captain's office is a coat of those very same regimentals I wore for my brief and dishonorable army career. I stare at the familiar royal blue and buff and brace myself for the usual winks and nudges. The coat hangs over a chair; of its owner there is no sign until a door, cunningly concealed by wallpaper, opens, and a complete stranger enters the room. He is only a few years older than I, a handsome, dark fellow, and possibly he served abroad for the twenty-odd hours of my military experience.

We bow, and I introduce myself to him. He doesn't turn a hair upon hearing my name. Possibly a whoremonger learns discretion in these matters. I agree to a ruinous interest rate, offer my diamond stickpin as surety, and pray that Terrant never hears of this particular aspect of the evening's adventures.

Miss Wellesley-Clegg

". . . And you see, I twisted this length of fabric together with a length of braid and a paste brooch, and then took the feathers from a bonnet I had . . ."

"It's most handsome," Kate says.

But before I can continue the description of my headdress, Inigo returns. He stops and stares at Kate; the extraordinary thing is that after the initial shock when she first undressed, and after a slightly awkward moment when she offered to unhook our gowns, we have got along famously. We hardly notice her nakedness, and, since the room is so warm, I am sure she is more comfortable than we are.

"Why, sir, we have been waiting for you." Kate's voice is now low and throaty. She rises to her knees and reaches for Inigo's coat buttons. His eyes become somewhat vacant.

"Inigo!" Julia says in an awful voice, even more stern than the one she used when Inigo almost unhooked Kate's gown.

Inigo seems to come back to life again. He backs away from Kate and tosses her gown at her. "Never mind that, my girl. Get dressed. These ladies are from the Association for the Rescue and Succor of those in Extremis."

She slips the gown over her head and smirks. "Oh, you mean A.R.S.E."

Oh, surely not. Celia, Julia, and I glance at each other in horror.

"Well, that's how all the gentlemen refer to it," Kate says, with an apologetic shrug, straightening her skirts.

Julia is the first to gain her equilibrium. "It does *not* spell that—that word."

Inigo shrugs. He does not look nearly as ashamed as he should. "Well, ah, not exactly. The *Association* for the *Rescue* and *Succor* of those in *Extremis*, you see . . . Those of vulgar taste find it amusing."

"It is not at all funny." I am furious. "You mean, you and Terrant and other gentlemen have known of this all along, and you have made fun of us? It is no wonder we cannot find a sponsor. Why did you not tell us of this before?"

Inigo shrugs. "Well, I . . . I thought you knew. I tried to persuade you to change the name, but . . ."

Above our heads a bed creaks with great vigor and a steady sense of rhythm, an unseemly reminder of what goes on in this elegantly-furnished house.

To distract myself I take one of the bottles of champagne and fiddle with the cork. As Inigo reaches for a glass, a flood of foam rushes over my hands.

Inigo clears his throat.

"We could leave you and the gentleman here, miss, if you wish," Kate says, her bosom carelessly falling out of her gown. "The sheets are hardly used at all this early in the evening."

I down a glass of wine rather fast. I wish I could feel more shocked at the suggestion, but I regret to say it has a certain appeal.

"About the Association, Kate," I say. "We . . ."

From the room next door comes the sound of slaps, female giggles, and a man's voice. "Oh, I am a most dreadful sinner, my dear. You must punish me severely."

Kate giggles. "The Bishop is at it again."

"At what? What on earth are they doing?"

"Peggy is whipping him, miss. You can look through the spyhole if you wish."

"Whipping him? Why should she do that? What spyhole?" I am horribly confused. I drink another glass of wine.

Kate glances at Inigo. "The gentleman will explain it all to you, miss, I am certain."

"Oh." I am alarmed that in only a few moments Kate has

ascertained the attraction beween me and Inigo. I hope it is her profession that makes her so perceptive.

"Inigo," Julia whispers to him, "I think we should leave immediately. I fear Philomena will be corrupted."

A footman enters with more lobster and oysters and another couple of bottles.

"Oh, you are a wicked boy!" cries the lightskirt from next door and His Grace howls with pain.

Celia cracks open a lobster claw. "Well, should we not ask her?"

"Yes, of course." I pour everyone more champagne. "Kate, we should like to offer you the chance to leave this life of depravity."

"Well, that's very kind of you, miss, but you see I'm quite happy here."

"But you can't possibly—why, you have to . . ." Celia goes quite pink. She devours a large chunk of lobster. "You know . . . with gentlemen."

"Oh, I don't mind it that much, miss. I usually think of something pleasant while the gentleman does his business, and you learn to get them off fast. If it is someone I fancy, then I enjoy myself, too." She gives Inigo a sidelong look.

"And where do you think you'll be in five years, or even two years?" Julia asks her.

"Dead, or running my own house, my lady." Her words are defiant, but she reminds me of a cardplayer placing a bet he cannot possibly win.

I sit beside her on the bed and take her hand; too late it strikes me that she may see my gesture as something else entirely. "Kate, you are so brave. But I should like to offer you a job where you could make forty pounds a year."

Kate laughs. "I make that in a quarter year or less, miss, and that's mostly on my back, and with that greedy Mrs. Bright taking most of the money."

"You would have safety, security, and a respectable profession."

"Miss, I had a respectable profession. I made a few shillings a week, working sixteen hours a day in a basement where the walls streamed water. That's how you ladies get your pretty gowns. And then I was ill, and my job gone. I'm fortunate that Mrs. Bright took me in."

What can I say to this? That I am sorry? Even I can see that would be an insult. Or an arrogant claim that our much-mocked Association intends to change the world? Instead I say, "I should like you to train as my maid."

There is a silence, or at least silence of a sort as the creaking from upstairs accelerates, and next door, loud groans replace the sound of a switch upon flesh.

"I don't think so, miss." She shakes her head, takes my hand, and gives it a kind squeeze. She, this woman who has nothing, is being kind to me, an heiress who has everything. Her grace and generosity astound me.

"You would do well to consider it, Kate." Julia sounds as though she is ordering a servant to sweep the floor.

We ignore her.

"Will you please give it some thought?" I pat her hand. "Here is one of my papa's cards. My name is Philomena Wellesley-Clegg."

"One of those Wellesleys? No? Well, thank you kindly, miss. I shall think about it."

We open a couple more bottles of champagne, Celia finishes the oysters, and we are all in very good spirits, apart from Inigo, who stands apart from us, frowning.

Kate meanwhile leaves the room and returns shortly with a bonnet and some sewing things. "I thought, miss—for they always say in the newspaper how you are in the very pink of fashion—that you might like to advise me on this bonnet. Gowns I know, but I don't have much reason to go outside, so . . ."

"Oh, what a sweet bonnet!" I pluck a couple of battered flowers from its brim and reach for my own headdress. "These feathers would look splendid on it."

"Maybe we should leave," Inigo suggests.

We all ignore him.

Julia relents and comes to join us, pulling silk flowers from her hair. "Kate, you can add in a small bunch of flowers here, and . . ."

Celia has been rather quiet—well, there was quite a lot of lobster for her to deal with—but now she stands and clutches her stomach. "Oh dear, I feel most unwell."

She looks quite dreadful, pale and sweaty.

"Inigo, leave the room," Julia says.

Our millinery project is abandoned as we comfort Celia, who is indeed dreadfully unwell—it must have been the lobster—and, heavens, we discover in the worst possible way how much she has consumed.

"I am afraid she is too ill to travel," Julia says to me in a whisper. "But she cannot stay here. Oh, Philomena, what shall we do?"

I glance at Celia, who lies pale and flat on the bed while

Kate wipes her face with a damp towel. "Maybe we should try to get her downstairs."

After a while we manage to do so, poor Celia limp and moaning as we support her.

Inigo waits for us there, and looks horrified. "Julia, she must stay at our house. It's closer. We'll send word to her family."

"Very well, and then you may escort Philomena home."

"It's not proper." This strikes me as a rather odd thing to say considering our activities tonight and Julia tells him, to my great delight, not to be a ninny.

We help poor Celia into the carriage, where the motion makes her exceedingly unwell again, and we have to stop three times in the course of the ten-minute drive so she may disgorge more bad lobster. Each time Inigo and the driver keep watch to make sure ruffians do not attack us. And I am dreadfully aware of how much I have drunk in the course of the evening—I am quite silly and find that even though I am sorry for Celia, part of me wants to giggle long and loud at our predicament.

It is indeed a relief to arrive at the Terrants' house, where Julia sends for her maid and housekeeper as well as several more footmen.

And then I am alone in the carriage with a man who has taken me to a house of ill repute, has poured me many glasses of champagne, and is moreover wearing very tight satin breeches.

"Oops, another sixpence."

"I beg your pardon?"

"It's a joke. A very private joke. I shan't tell you."

He nods. This is most unlike Inigo, who usually has something to say, so I decide I must initiate polite conversation.

"Inigo, why did that woman beat the Bishop?"

Oh dear, not particularly polite.

He looks very uncomfortable and clears his throat, something he has done a lot tonight. I do hope he is not catching a cold. "Ah. Some men find it arousing."

"Really? Why? Do you?"

"No."

The carriage lurches forward, depositing me quite neatly onto his lap.

But of course he is a gentleman; there is nothing to fear.

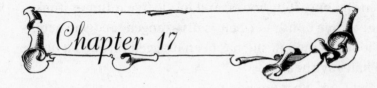

Chapter 17

Mr. Inigo Linsley

Tonight I am not a gentleman.

I know there is no excuse for what happens next. We are both foxed, I have spent the day in some discomfort as Philomena caresses nude male statues in front of me, and then I have been treated to an abundance of female flesh as Kate displayed her not unattractive wares.

In a word, I am primed, and Philomena, although she does not realize it, is too.

So when she lands on my lap, soft and fragrant and giggling—her person, that is, not my lap which is anything but soft—in the dark intimacy of the hackney, I react as any man would.

I shall not go into any vulgar details. Suffice it to say that when I taste the fascinating hollow at her collarbone, she hums and purrs like a cat, arching against me. Furthermore, the gown with which Philomena flaunts her charms fastens by only four hooks, and in the five minutes it takes to get to her house her hair is disarranged, and she generally looks as though she has been dragged through a hedge and half-ravished.

Good God, what am I doing?

She has not been idle, and my neckcloth is in ruins and my shirt half out of my breeches.

"Oh! We're home!" She giggles as I attempt to make her look decent.

Somehow she has lost a slipper and I fumble, swearing mightily, on the floor of the carriage in the dark.

"Thank you for a most interesting evening, Mr. Linsley," she says for the footman's benefit as I hand her into the house. "I do like your breeches. Oops. Another sixpence."

Miss Philomena Wellesley-Clegg

Oh, I shall die. I feel so dreadfully unwell.

"Why, miss, Mr. Linsley is a passionate man indeed," Hen says as she brushes my hair, which is a tangled bush. I am not yet dressed, and I see in the mirror, at the neckline of my shift, a red mark. It is in fact not at my neck, nor even my shoulder, although there is a similar mark there, too, but much lower down, lower even than the pink dress.

Hen dabs witchhazel and arnica onto my skin.

Inigo has marked me. Inigo's mouth. I have hot, shameful

memories of our journey home, and now I am horrified.

"Hold your tongue, Hen."

"Beg your pardon, miss. I daresay the marriage will be put forward." Hen grins. *"And the gates of pearl and gold . . ."*

Fortunately I am dressed by the time Mama enters the room, babbling of the ball, threatening me with the rigors of a visit from the dressmaker, and mentions in passing that Mr. Linsley is here to bid me farewell.

Farewell?

Then I remember he is off to Weaselcopse Manor today, and my headache and misery increase.

He awaits me in the drawing room, and I know I look a frowsty fright, in a morning dress that has never suited me, and I wonder why I chose that particular print. Its colors hurt my eyes. Everything hurts my eyes, even Inigo, who wears breeches (another sixpence) and boots for his trip into the country, and looks handsome and lively.

"Well, Philomena, you look rather the worse for wear."

"That is not a gallant thing to say, sir."

"But a true one. Here, my manservant makes this up for me, and it will do you a power of good." He hands me a silver flask.

I take a sip. It tastes disgusting, and I fear for a moment I shall cast my accounts onto his boots again. The stuff burns my mouth, and I gulp down a cup of tea in one mouthful—I am dreadfully thirsty, too—and feel slightly better.

"Thank you. What was in that?"

"It's a secret remedy."

"Inigo, about last night . . ." My face heats. Should I tell him he doesn't have to marry me after what we did? Do we need to marry? And what did we do, exactly? Sudden, startling images flash into my mind—my hand under his shirt, the smooth skin and curling hair. And his hands. Dear God. And his mouth.

"I beg your pardon. I was very ungentlemanly, but you behaved in a most ladylike manner."

"Oh. Did I?" Now I am even more confused. Do all ladies allow gentlemen to unhook their gowns and kiss them like that?

"Indeed, yes." He nods in a way that does not entirely convince me. "Philomena, I think you know what I am about to say. As you know I am going into the country to oversee repairs on the cottage on my estate. But now, following a conversation I have had with Mrs. Gibbons, it is imperative I see to the manor house itself. You see—"

The door opens and Lydia and Charlotte enter the room. Oh, the tiresome things. They curtsey to Inigo and plant themselves on the sofa next to me.

"Mama said we should practice our social graces," Lydia says.

"The weather has been very fine lately," Charlotte says.

Rain streams down the windows.

"I read in the newspaper this morning that—"

"Miss Charlotte, Miss Lydia, it is charming to see you again," Inigo says. "Would you like to play the pianoforte for us?"

"Yes, Mr. Linsley."

To my relief they retire to the instrument and bang out a duet, accompanied by a discussion on whether they should take the repeats.

"Philomena, as I was about to say, Fanny—Mrs. Gibbons—has—"

Mama, all smiles, enters the drawing room. "Why Mr. Linsley how delightful for you to call as I was saying only just now to Mr. Wellesley-Clegg you should dine with us soon but I hear you are to go to the country well that is a shame indeed but just listen to my two dear girls do not they play with exquisite taste—"

"F-sharp, dimwit!" shrieks Lydia as the music stumbles to a discordant halt.

After a brief pause the duet resumes with the grace of a trayful of china falling down the stairs.

"Ladies." Inigo rises. "I must leave you. My coach departs soon. Philomena, there is something I must say to you."

I accompany him into the hall, where our footman hands him his hat and stick. I stare at him, sick at heart.

He is to marry her.

He wishes to release me from the engagement, and I thought this was what I wanted, too. Now I don't know what I want.

I think about how he calls me a ninny far too often.

I remember how frightened and then how angry he was when I fell off Blaze. How when he tucked the pug-scented shawl around me in my aunt's barouche his voice was full of kindness and concern, and the safety I felt in his arms. And the equally wonderful danger in those same arms last night.

I whisper the only thing I can under the circumstances. "I understand. Of course this false engagement may end at any time. That was always our agreement."

"Dearest Philomena, that is precisely the point I wished to make."

The footman opens the door.

I raise my chin and offer him my hand. I smile. I am not sure how I manage to do it, but my reflection in the hall mirror seems quite satisfactory. I may as well remind him he is not my only chance. "I am sure I shall receive an offer soon. I have great hopes of Almack's tonight. Everyone says I must be snapped up soon, and there is a wager on me at White's."

He has raised my hand halfway to his lips, but stops. "I see. I shall wish you good hunting, then, Miss Wellesley-Clegg."

He steps out into the rain.

He'll get even wetter if he travels outside on the coach, but he is no longer of any concern to me.

I sink into a chair in the hall.

I will not cry.

Mr. Inigo Linsley

She was flirting with me.

Surely that was what she meant.

Thank God I have a sensible woman like Mrs. Gibbons in my life, who, when I went to visit her and Will earlier this morning, told me in no uncertain terms what I should do—marry Philomena as soon as possible and drop this idiocy of a false engagement.

Rain pours down, the coach rocks and lurches, and the umbrella of the man seated next to me tips chilly water down my neck. Yes, I had an inside ticket, but gave it to a young woman with a baby of about Will's age who was to travel outside.

She blushed scarlet and scrambled into the coach, stammering her thanks, while the others with inside tickets scowled at me for setting an infant in their midst.

I turn up the collar of my greatcoat and consider Philomena. Didn't she realize I was about to propose to her before her sisters, her mother, and that damned footman intervened? I curse myself for my procrastination, and, to be honest, my cowardice. I could, after all, have dragged her into the water-closet, butler's pantry, coal-hole, or some other convenient nook for an honest proposal.

Philomena, my beloved Philomena. I thought her an empty-headed, silly little thing at first, and I am quite sure she thought no better of me.

She loves me, I have no doubt of it.

I imagine her at Almack's, flirting with determination, wearing one of her delightful gowns. That Darrowby fellow had me somewhat concerned, but I believe Philomena regards him as a sort of brother, and it is a strange thing, that women tend to discard the decent man beneath their noses for the lure of an adventurer or rake. Why they think such a man will turn over a new leaf after a parson has babbled for a couple of minutes is a mystery. However, since I have not achieved truly great distinction in the realms of depravity, I am more than willing to learn to be a decent fellow for Philomena.

I wish I had known about the wager at White's. Some very determined gentlemen will be after my sweet Philomena, and I don't like it.

I almost jump off the coach and rush back to London to propose to her again.

No, I shall not. I shall let her enjoy herself.

As we leave the grime and smoke of London behind us, the rain stops, and the sun comes out, hedgerows and trees alight with sparkling drops of rain. It is an omen, I am sure of it.

Miss Wellesley-Clegg

I am quite low for the rest of the day, and Mama, Papa, and Hen treat me with great kindness, which only makes me feel worse.

My mood improves slightly when I put on my new lavender gown, with a silk overskirt and train, and a most beautiful trim at the hem in silver and purple. Hen made me lie down in the afternoon with slices of cucumber on my eyes, and now I look very well, and the prospect of an evening of dancing and flirting, even if it is at Almack's, does not seem quite so bad. The rain has stopped, too, so I am not quite so worried about damage to my slippers or my gown.

I do not need Inigo's presence to make me happy.

I am glad the pretence and deception are over, that is all.

Almack's is as dreary and stiff as usual, but Julia takes me aside and tells me some delightful news. She wants me to be a godmother! And she very much admires my gown.

But it is not enough to lighten my mood.

I attract much attention from gentlemen, which is most gratifying. Yet I find them mostly insipid. Oh, what is wrong with me? Am I catching a cold, or a consumption, or colic?

I do hope not. I want to be well when Inigo returns, for I should hate him to think I fell into a decline as soon as he told me he was to marry Mrs. Gibbons. I repeat the words to myself: *He is to marry Mrs. Gibbons. He is to marry Mrs. Gibbons.* Repeat anything often enough and it becomes a meaningless jumble of sounds; eventually I shall be able to say those six words without pain. I am determined it shall be so.

So I smile and make polite conversation, dance every dance, and watch the clock. And then, when it is the last dance before suppertime, Lady Jersey condescends to introduce me to a gentleman I have not seen before.

"Captain Horatio Blackwater at your service, ma'am." He bows low and kisses my hand.

When he straightens up, my eyes are on a direct level with the gold coat buttons of his regimentals. I tilt my head back and see a noble, dark countenance, with expressive, flashing eyes, and tumbled, heroic waves of black hair.

He is quite the most god-like creature I have ever seen.

He still holds my hand.

Mr. Linsley was never really quite tall enough for my tastes—taller than Papa but not as tall as Tom Darrowby.

This gentleman will do very well.

Mr. Inigo Linsley

Reasons I should marry Miss Wellesley-Clegg

1. She is a shocking flirt and will break the heart of every bachelor in town if I do not intervene.

2. I do not want any other gentleman teaching her about men.

3. Ditto kissing her.

4. Ditto unfastening any of those scandalous gowns she favors.

5. Her papa tolerates me, I have learned to insinuate conversation into her mama's babble, and her younger sisters do not alarm me quite as much now.

6. She likes Will and Fanny.

7. She loves me, I am quite sure.

8. I love her.

9. I love her.

10. I love her.

I can scarcely wait to see her again. Seated atop the coach—it is a fine day, and a pleasure to sit outside—I grasp a basket of eggs to my chest and grin like a fool. I do not care that I look like a country bumpkin. I probably have straw in my hair, and my coat, shared with a family of moths, is one of the old ones I keep at Weaselcopse Manor for working on the estate. I consider for a brief moment returning to our house to change into town clothes, but my ardor knows no bounds.

I take a hackney to the Wellesley-Cleggs' house, and the

traffic in London has never seemed slower. I trust she is not out buying herself more silly bonnets. I imagine her engaged at home on genteel pursuits, mending her stockings—that arouses some very ungentlemanly thoughts in my head; possibly sighing over a book of poetry—I imagine the sweet turn of her lips as she reads; or playing the pianoforte, her little fingers skittering over the keys like mice.

This must be love. I have certainly turned into a sentimental fool.

After a few centuries of travel I arrive and am admitted into the drawing room, where I place my basket of eggs on the sideboard.

Philomena flings open the door and gives me one of her adorably sweet smiles. "Oh, Inigo, I am so glad to see you!"

"And I you." I restrain myself from kissing her. I don't want to alarm her.

"Papa said I should talk to you."

"Why? Philomena, my love . . ." I grasp her hands in mine.

"Inigo, I trust you will be happy for me."

What the devil does she say?

"You see . . ." She blushes most becomingly. "I wish to release you from our engagement."

Chapter 18

Miss Philomena Wellesley-Clegg

Inigo's face is quite pale all of a sudden.

"You want to do *what*?" he says after a very long pause.

"I have received an offer of marriage."

"Who is it?" His jaw is very tight and his eyes fierce.

"Why do you wish to know?" I am becoming less comfortable by the moment.

"So I may kill him."

I truly believe, from the look in his eyes, that he will.

"Inigo, this was our arrangement, and after our last conversation—"

"Arrangement be damned!"

"I am desperately in love with him." That really didn't sound quite passionate enough. Will I sound foolish if I repeat it while sighing and casting my eyes to the ceiling?

He releases my hands which he has held quite tightly all this time. "You love him."

"Yes."

"I see."

In the silence that ensues, my uncertainty turns to confusion.

He told me he was going to marry Mrs. Gibbons.

Didn't he?

And then I am angry. Angry that he threw his mistress and his b—d son in my face, and unhooked my dress and kissed me in a most disrespectful manner; and angry at myself that I enjoyed it far too much. Angry that he loved another woman and not me.

"Well, what did you expect? Besides, sir, your affections are engaged elsewhere, as you have clearly made plain to me."

"Indeed? And who is the lucky woman?" He sounds angry, now, too, and I fear what we are about to do to each other.

"It is Mrs. Gibbons, as you know well. You told me as much when you were here, that she had agreed to marry you—"

"I *what*?" He stares at me in bewilderment, or a good imitation thereof.

"You told me—" My voice croaks. I clear my throat and start again. "You told me you had spoken with her, I presume that very morning, for if it was not, then what you did to me in the carriage the previous night was even more depraved—"

"What I did to you? You were perfectly willing, as I remember."

He stands there a moment, fists clenched, as though collecting his thoughts. "Philomena—Miss Wellesley-Clegg—I spoke with Mrs. Gibbons that morning. I visited my son; naturally she was there too. She advised me that I should ask my future wife if she were willing to have my former mistress and our child live half a mile from my house, on my estate. That is all."

"But you said—you said you were to marry her." Didn't he?

He looks down his nose—he is quite tall enough to do that. He drawls, all languid, *ton* arrogance, "I think Mr. Gibbons might have something to say on the matter."

So it is an adulterous liaison! He is truly depraved!

"Wipe that maidenly shock from your face, you ninny," he says.

"Don't call me a ninny!" I fairly bellow at him, the way I shout at my younger sisters.

"She married him when she was fifteen, they lived together for some three months, and she has not seen him since. And, yes, we have a child, but she does not love me, and although I have proposed marriage, has rejected me each time. I love you, Philomena, although I must be a fool to do so."

"Oh, thank you very much!"

"I love you," he repeats.

I had supposed, that if I were to force him to declare his feelings for me that I would feel triumphant, vindicated. Instead, I feel quite dreadful.

"I'm sorry. I did not mean . . ."

"Oh, please, Miss Wellesley-Clegg. You knew perfectly well what you were about. I have no need of your pity. I was a fool, and that is the end of it." He advances on me then, and I am quite fearful of what I see in his face, and at the same time, to my shame, quite thrilled.

He backs me up against the sideboard, and his voice is low and dangerous. "Just remember one thing, Miss Wellesley-Clegg. Whoever he is, he'll not love you as I do. He won't kiss you the way I do, and you'll regret you turned me down. You'll regret it for the rest of your life."

Before I can remind him there was nothing to turn down since he was too careless to bother with a real proposal, I can move back no further and he reminds me of exactly why I entered into this sham engagement in the first place.

I am incapable of thought as his mouth closes over mine, but one sentiment rages in my head: that he is right. No one else can possibly make me feel weak and soft and silly and at the same time as though I am burning up, and all from his mouth on mine. And at the same time I know that he has nothing to lose, he kisses me as though his life depended upon it, and although I should be indifferent, I am not.

My legs begin to give way and I clutch wildly with one hand for support. My fingers grasp something woven and woody.

As he releases me, the basket falls to the floor and eggs break all over the floor in a flood of smashed shells.

"Good-bye, Philomena. I wish you well."

And I stand there, with broken eggs lapping at my feet, and watch him go.

It's very quiet. There's the occasional quiet splintering sound of a broken eggshell settling, and a crunch when I move one of my feet.

"Well, miss, I don't know why it is he makes such a mess when he comes to our house. First the paint, and now this."

"Oh, Hen." I hadn't even heard her come in. Maybe I should fling myself into her arms.

Maybe not. She looks at me with cool disapproval. "You know what they say about a girl and broken eggs, don't you, miss?" Now there's a slight smirk on her face.

I shake my head, no.

Hen leans toward me. "They say it's her virtue gone. All I can say is, miss, you were lucky he arrived when he did, with the captain talking to the master in his study."

She's right. It could have been blood on the floor, not broken eggs. "Why are you being so unpleasant, Hen?"

"I like Mr. Linsley," she says. The impertinence, as if my choice of suitors were of any concern to her. "And for all the captain's a military hero, there's something I don't trust about him, and I've said as much to your mama, and your papa, too. Old Hen looks out for you, miss, and don't you forget it."

"Pray clean the floor," I say in as dignified a tone as possible, and attempt to sweep from the room—almost impossible, as my egg-soaked stockings squish in my shoes. I catch a glimpse of my reflection in the hall mirror, and I look shockingly bad—my face is all red, and my hair is in complete disorder.

Oh horrors, the doorknob to Papa's study turns. They will be out in a moment, and I am not fit to be seen. I have no choice but to dive into the water-closet where Inigo first proposed to me and hold my breath for a number of reasons.

"Good God, Hen, what's this?" I hear Papa say. "And where's Miss Philly?"

"In the water closet, sir." Oh, I could kill her. I truly could. To admit that in front of the gentleman to whom I am now engaged!

"She had an accident with some eggs." Oh, that sounds even worse. I am mortified.

"So I see. Come, Blackwater, we'll go to the morning room instead. You'll get to meet my two youngest girls. I regret you can't yet meet my son Robert—he's busy looking after things for us at home . . ."

Papa's voice dies away as he leads my dearest Horatio away, and when all is quiet I tiptoe out of the water-closet, squelch upstairs, wash my feet, and change my gown. I splash cold water on my face and tie my hair back with a ribbon. I leave the gown and ruined slippers and stockings in a heap on the floor for Hen to sort out. I need to look innocent and untouched, as though I have not just kissed someone while engaged—or almost engaged—to another. As though doubts do not rage in my mind.

Oh, nonsense. I shall be Mrs. Horatio Blackwater. I shall live happily ever after. I do wonder where we shall live, but doubtless Horatio will find us a charming country place, not too far from Mama and Papa. Or we shall live in style in London and attend all the most fashionable soirees, al- though quite honestly why one should wish to do so, having obtained a husband, is a mystery. I should much prefer staying at home with my dear husband, although I am not sure quite what we'd talk about. But of course, we'd read poetry aloud to each other by a cosy fireside. I shall embroider something exquisite. A baby's cap, for instance.

Oh, it will be delightful.

Absolutely delightful.

I am the happiest of women.

Devoid of egg, I go downstairs, endeavoring to put a girlish spring into my step. The footman in the hall, carrying a bucket and mop, asks me if I am feeling all right, for my gait seems unsteady.

"Oh, I am quite well, Simon. I am engaged now."

"Why, congratulations, miss. Mr. Linsley was most generous to us concerning the matter of the blue paint."

"Not to Mr. Linsley!" I hiss like an enraged serpent.

"Beg your pardon, miss. It's the captain, then, is it?"

"Yes."

He gives me a dour nod. "Much happiness, miss."

I shall really have to talk to Papa about the servants' impertinence. First Hen, and now Simon. It is too bad.

Everyone—Mama, Papa, my sisters, and Horatio—look up when I enter the morning room. Papa and Horatio, of course, stand, and Papa comes over to me and kisses me. "Is everything all right, lass?" he murmurs under the flow of Mama's chatter.

"Why, yes, Papa." I hope my carefree laugh doesn't sound as much of a wild cackle as it does to my ears.

"Any doubts, Philly, and you don't have to have him. You know that."

"No, Papa." For a moment I wish I could pour my heart out to him, if I could even put into words the emotions I feel at the moment.

"Why now Philly oh doesn't she look well my dearest Horatio I believe I may safely call you that now oh it is so delightful come my dears you must help me with something upstairs Lydia pray bring my sewing box . . ." She bears my sisters away in a tide of chatter.

Papa shakes Horatio's hand and leaves.

For the first time we are alone in a room together.

He raises my hand to his lips and kisses it, while gazing at me with his dark, dark eyes—like bottomless pools of water, and his eyelashes like overhanging ferns, although of course not green.

"Did Papa ask you about subsidence?"

"Subsidence, my darling?" His voice is rich and warm like chocolate.

"Yes. It's one of his main interests, because of the mine. And the house. You know our house is falling down because of it." I gulp in some air.

"You are altogether charming, Philly."

"Don't call me Philly!" I snatch my hand back. How dare he!

"I beg your pardon. I thought since your family address you so, it was your preference."

"No. I hate it." And what right does he have to think he can address me by my Christian name? Or that loathed shortened version of it?

He takes my hand again. "I should like to claim a kiss, now we are betrothed."

Oh. I knew this would happen. A kiss. And of course it will be wonderful.

He winds one arm around my waist so I am pressed against a quantity of gold frogging and lowers his mouth to mine. Of course he is so much taller that he has to hunch over a little, even though I stand on tiptoes, and I feel we must look foolish together.

He has something on his hair, or his skin, maybe, that smells odd. His mouth is cool and encloses mine completely so I fear for a moment I shall not be able to breathe. And then something thick and wet pushes inside my mouth, and it feels like an invasion, not an act of tenderness.

I pull away and I am afraid my face reveals my repulsion.

He laughs. "Your maidenly modesty becomes you, my dear Philomena." He leans to whisper in my ear, "I admit I am impatient to taste your charms. What say you to a special licence?"

Impatient to taste your charms? It reminds me of Mrs. Bright commanding Kate to raise her skirts. "You must talk to Papa."

"Of course." He places one hand on my bodice. I wish I could say the hand was on my shoulder, but it is not my shoulder at all, somewhat further down, and certainly a place no gentleman would place his hand (although one has and I am guiltily aware of that fact. But he is no gentleman and I will not think of him).

Oh lord, Blackwater is as bad as Elverton and his cow. No, he is worse. He squeezes.

I give a small stifled squeak of alarm and feel most foolish. "I think Mama may need my help," I blurt out, and bolt from the room.

Mr. Inigo Linsley

Stairs. A lot of them. Some marble, cool against my face when I found myself lying on them. Cards, too, sliding from my hands as though bewitched, the idiot grins of the kings and queens and jacks mocking me. And claret, dear God, rivers and rivers of claret, and I the conduit through which it has passed.

Church bells clang nearby, or inside my head, I can't tell, and I don't want to know.

I am ill. Deathly ill.

I can still breathe, which I do with some misgiving. Eyes closed, I take stock of my surroundings. All limbs appear to be present although I am completely unclothed. The sheets are warm and soft and smell better than I. I move my hands around. I am alone.

Good. One embarrassment spared.

But where am I?

I can hear the sounds of traffic, street cries, and those damnable bells, faintly muffled. Closer still, is the sound of a baby's babble, and a woman's voice. Ever conscious of my roiling insides, I smell coffee nearby.

I open my eyes. Shards of light pierce my skull and I close them again. I try again, and find myself gazing at a canopy, stuff of dark blue with a shiny stripe in the same color. I remember when she chose that for our bed. The bed from Mr. Totterton's shop. This bed.

Dear God.

I close my eyes and release a heartfelt groan.

The door opens and closes, and I hear her footsteps, light and quick on the wooden floor.

"So you're awake." Her voice is impatient, a busy woman who has things to do and not much time to deal with the drunken wretch in her bed.

I make a sound. Once I had the power of speech, but apparently now it is lost to me.

"Fanny," I manage to say.

"Here, take this. Open your eyes, Inigo."

"Dadadadada," says my son.

I open my eyes. He is perched on Fanny's hip, his little legs kicking. He reaches for me. Me, the drunken dissolute who has crawled back into his mother's bed. Yet he loves me still.

"Inigo!" She shoves a cup of coffee at me.

I manage to raise myself onto one elbow and drink the coffee, very strong and sweet. There is a moment of indecision while my stomach debates whether this is the final insult, to be expelled immediately, or whether it should be accepted as a peace offering. I am happy to say it is the latter.

"Well," says Fanny. She sits at the end of the bed, well out of grabbing range, and frowns at me. "And can you speak?"

I make another sound.

She takes the cup from my limp fingers, leaves the room, and returns a few moments later with more coffee.

"Thank you," I manage to say this time.

She takes the empty coffee cup, places it well out of reach, and puts Will onto the bed. Babbling, he crawls toward me, sweet-smelling and delighted to see me. At my chest, he stops to examine a feature he is familiar with, although of far more use and beauty on his mother.

"Careful, Will," I say as he reaches out with thumb and finger like a little crab, a look of intense concentration on his face.

He seems impressed by my anatomy and replaces his fingers with his mouth, sucking like the devil. I give a yell of pain and he bursts into tears.

"Oh, little lad, Papa's sorry," I take him in my arms, kissing his wet face. "Don't cry, Will."

Fanny gives a huff of annoyance and takes him from me, rocking him against her bosom. "So you've come back to life. Would you like some more coffee?"

"No, thank you. Fanny, did we . . . that is to say, last night, when I . . ." I have only the haziest recollections of the previous evening. God knows what I have done. Is a brother or sister for little Will growing inside her even now?

Will struggles from Fanny's arms and crawls on the bed, babbling and cooing.

"Oh, sir." Fanny lowers her eyelashes. "Never shall I forget last night. It was . . . never have I known you more potent, your ardor so unflagging, your engine of love more mighty."

I cover my innocent son's ears with my hands.

She continues, "I blush to remember the acts we performed. My screams of passion were intermixed with pleas as I begged you for more, more, and you rose to the occasion again and again—"

"Now, Fanny—"

"You drove me to heights of ecstasy hitherto unscaled by woman. Why, today I can scarcely walk. I am the envy of my female neighbors—"

"Fanny, you're funning me, I hope."

This is apparently the wittiest thing anyone has ever said to her. She hoots with laughter, for what I consider an inordinately long time, and Will looks at her and laughs too.

"Inigo, you fool," she says, "you walked in here at two in the morning, announced your heart was broken, and took off all your clothes. Then you got into bed."

"And that was all?"

She snorts. "Do you think you would have been capable of anything more? My guests were somewhat astonished."

"Your guests?" Oh, good God. Did I strip in front of complete strangers? Or worse, people I know?

"When I saw what you were about, I brought you in here. You looked already quite foolish enough."

"And then what?"

"After a while, I came to bed, too. You hardly stirred all night. And that was all."

"Oh, thank God. That is to say, Fan . . . well, you know what I mean."

"It's a good thing I do." She allows me to kiss her hand. "And do you want to tell me about this business of your broken heart?"

"You can probably guess the matter."

She nods. "I'm sorry, Inigo."

"It won't affect our arrangement. The cottage is ready . . ."

She silences me with a fingertip on my mouth. "Hush," she says as tenderly as though she spoke to Will.

"Where's my coat?"

"In the other room. Why, were you playing cards?"

"I'm afraid so. I feel strong enough to view the damage."

She leaves me and Will while she fetches my coat, and we

look through the pockets. To my astonishment, my pockets are full of notes and IOUs from others—I barely remember the card games, much less winning.

"Fifteen hundred guineas," Fanny says. Will crawls back to her and she kisses his head.

"How absurd. I never win at cards."

"Only sober and with a whole heart you don't." She hesitates. "Inigo, would you like me to talk to Philomena? I liked her so much, and I thought she suited you well."

"She's found someone else. It was her prerogative. At the time I didn't think either of us cared. But I do."

"I hate to see you unhappy, Inigo. Who is he?"

"I don't know. She wouldn't tell me his name after I threatened to kill him."

We both become aware that Will is silent, and with a baby of his age, that is never a good sign.

Will sits with a beatific smile on his face, and shreds of paper dangling from his mouth. More fragments, damp and ruined, are clutched in his hands. He opens his mouth and releases an aristocratic and expensive smear in ink as a gray, gooey mess.

My lovely son has just eaten my winnings.

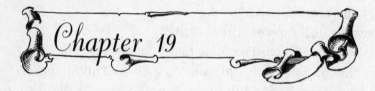

Chapter 19

Madam,

I return herein the sum of seventeen shillings and sixpence that you were obliging enough to donate to the Association for the Rescue and Succor of those in Extremis. I thank you for your term as Secretary and must inform you your services are no longer required in this or any other capacity.

I offer my congratulations on your engagement, and remain your most faithful servant,

Julia Linsley

Mr. Inigo Linsley

I return to a house full of tears. Julia, it appears, has succumbed to her condition, and lies on a sofa, crying. My mother, embroidering with fury, stabbing her needle into the cloth with some violence, occupies another.

"What did you *do*, Inigo?" Julia asks.

I shrug.

"I have lost my best friend," she wails.

"I too," snarls my mother from across the room, and brandishes a large pair of scissors at me.

I cannot bear this Greek chorus of lamenting recrimination, and leave to bump into my brother in the hall.

"I should have known," he says in disgust. "You'd best go to the country. I can't have you here upsetting the women."

"Yes, brother. I'll leave immediately."

"No. On Monday. Tonight is the Wellesley-Cleggs' ball."

"We have to go to that?"

He looks embarrassed. "Well, of course. Julia wants to give Philomena the cut direct, and she wants to see what she's wearing. Apparently there's some business of a new gown."

I just don't understand women. "But—but she's in there, crying like a baby."

"I know." He pats my shoulder. "I'm sorry, Ratsarse."

His small gesture of sympathy nearly undoes me. I rush away, seeking refuge and a razor. I briefly consider cutting my throat, then decide I will not give that faithless flirt the satisfaction of seeing the extent of my broken heart.

Janet Mullany

Miss Philomena Wellesley-Clegg

Nothing is going right. Hen is being deliberately uncooperative, we have two hours until guests arrive and I am still not dressed, my hair stands out like a wild bush and I cannot find my favorite fan.

"And the great pit of fire . . ." drones Hen. "You want this sewn in here, miss? You're quite sure?"

"Yes! That is the third time I have told you."

She smirks. *"Sinners all we cry to thee . . .*Well, it's a change from usual, miss, that's all."

"I'll tell Mama how contrary you are."

"Aye, miss, and I'll tell her how you told the dressmaker, when your mama wasn't listening, to cut the bodice lower than was decent."

"And so now I've changed my mind. Mama was right. You should be pleased. Oh, give it to me. I'll do it myself." I grab the gown from her, prick my finger, and a large blob of blood spills on the fabric. "Now see what you've done. I've ruined it."

"Give it to me, miss." She snatches it back and something rips.

At that moment, fortunately, someone raps on my door. "Philly? Are you dressed?"

I pull on a wrapper. "Come in, Papa."

He takes a look at me, red-faced and fighting tears, and holds out his arms. "Now, pet, what's the matter? Hen, you can leave us."

"Oh, Papa." I snivel wretchedly against his coat. "I think I may have made a mistake, becoming engaged to the captain."

"Indeed, lass. Why's that? Something you've heard about him? We don't have to announce it tonight, you know, although your mother's set on it."

I try to think of a way to tell my dear papa that my mistake is in choosing a man who cannot make me feel shivery and indecent and in whose breeches I have no interest. Oh, it's no good. I shrug instead.

"He is a bit of a dark horse," Papa says. "I've asked a few questions, you see. But if he's the one you want . . ."

I regret pride and modesty will not allow me to speak, and neither will Mama, who bursts into the room in full flood. "Oh my dear Mr. Wellesley-Clegg just look at this child she is not even dressed oh Philly have you been using the lotion I gave you and your hair it looks like a Medusa or a Myrmidon or some such I cannot remember these classical names and my dear child if you cry you will ruin your looks oh Philly my love every young lady becomes sentimental when she becomes engaged why the evening my engagement to Mr. Wellesley-Clegg was to be announced I ran upstairs and hid under my bed and my brothers had to pull me out and I was covered with dust for our housemaids were a sorry lot—"

"She'll do, Mrs. Wellesley-Clegg. She'll do." Papa pats my shoulder and I snort loudly into his handkerchief. "Our Philly will do us proud, you'll see."

I love Horatio.

I do not love Mr. Linsley.

"But there's something else," Papa says. "I received news from Robert that the main staircase at home has developed a sag of some six inches, and that's not good, not good at all.

Robert has propped it up, but I fear I must travel north as soon as possible and see the damage for myself."

"Oh, Papa! But you will stay tonight, I hope."

"Of course, my dear. I'll see the dancing and merry-making underway, and then leave, and come back as soon as possible. I don't want to miss my little girl's last days with us."

I look at my parents, who stand, hands clasped, and gaze at me with such pride and love, I vow not to let them down. They have already been distressed at my decision to end the engagement to Inigo, Mr. Linsley, I mean, and Mama wept long and bitter tears at the possibility that her newfound friendship with the Dowager Countess of Terrant was over.

It was Mr. Linsley's fault anyway.

"And just in case you need a few wedding gew-gaws, I thought you might like a little extra," Papa says. He produces a leather bag from inside his coat. "Fifty guineas should buy you a couple of bonnets, I think. Why, for all I know, I'll come back and find my little Philly a married woman."

"Oh, Papa!" I am overcome with gratitude at his generosity and kiss him so hard I nearly knock him over.

I swear I shall be a dutiful daughter from now on.

And from that point, everything goes well. Hen comes back with the gown, now pristine, mended and ironed, and with a piece of lace inserted in the bosom. I do not wish to appear immodest, and neither do I wish to drive Horatio mad with temptation. After all, we are expected to marry very soon. It is a pity the prospect fills me only with gloom.

Hen does something miraculous to my hair and my fan

turns up in my glove drawer. And so I am ready to make my grand entrance, and see all the *ton* there, and flirt and be admired.

And, oh yes, Horatio will be there too.

Mr. Inigo Linsley

Well fortified with claret I join my family for our foray into what is now enemy territory. We arrive late, of course. It is what the *ton* does. We stand at the top of the staircase leading down into the ballroom and view the ranks below.

I produce a quizzing-glass, borrowed for the occasion, and receive a haughty view of tiny, distorted figures.

"Wrong way round, Ratsarse," my brother Terrant says and plucks it away from me.

We are all astonished by the decoration of the room. It is Mrs. Wellesley-Clegg's speech personified, if that were possible—a never-ending riot of exuberantly-hued garlands, swags, Chinese lanterns, model pagodas, and strange artificial birds. The servants are dressed in exotic costumes covered in mirrors, paste jewels, and feathers. It is both vulgar and endearing.

"Most unusual," says my mama.

We Montagues make our aristocratic descent into the pit of Capulets, looking down our long noble noses like so many greyhounds.

Philomena and Mrs. Wellesley-Clegg move forward to greet us.

Julia turns her shoulder on them and walks away. It is

devilish rude; I didn't know she had it in her. Philomena blushes deep red and stares at her fan.

The Dowager Countess and the tradesman's wife look at each other like a couple of bulls across a meadow. My mama, I swear, paws the ground.

The room seems extraordinarily quiet, when in fact it is no such thing—it is merely one of those rare moments when Mrs. Wellesley-Clegg does not speak.

And then the two schoolgirls rush into each other's arms, knocking each other's headdresses askew, babbling that nothing shall ever come between them, and how all is forgiven and how unhappy they have been.

Julia, at a distance, stamps her foot.

"Good God. Women," says my brother. "Let's get a drink."

At that moment people gather for the next dance, and I lose sight of Philomena without having spoken a word to her, although I have no idea what I should say. As it's a country dance, I can't tell who her partner is, and she's short enough that she often disappears from view.

I make conversation with acquaintances and don't have the heart to join in the banter about the vulgarity of the room. I want only to look at Philomena, my Philomena, whose gown is cut halfway to her chin instead of her knees, and who looks far too happy for my liking.

And then I see him. He stands at the side of the room, and my first thought is that with all the gentlemen of the *ton* here tonight it must be a slow night at Mrs. Bright's. He too watches Philomena, and I don't like the expression on his face.

"What the devil is he doing here?" The words burst out of my mouth.

A gentleman nearby looks at me in astonishment. "Why, sir, that's Captain Horatio Blackwater of the –th. His engagement to Miss Wellesley-Clegg was announced earlier tonight."

Captain Horatio Blackwater of the –th! More like Captain Horatio Blackwater of the mounted fillies of Covent Garden. This is my rival! A whoremaster! What on earth does Mr. Wellesley-Clegg think he is about?

The dance ends, and I push my way through the crowd toward Philomena and the blackhearted Blackwater, but he whisks her away through a doorway—I grit my teeth at the thought of what he will do to her—and I become caught in a great crush of people.

I enquire urgently as to the whereabouts of Mr. Wellesley-Clegg, but no one seems to know where he is. Then, with a burst of brilliance, I make my way to the ladies' retiring room.

"Hen!" I shout, battering on the door, "Let me in!"

I am answered by a collection of female shrieks.

"I'll do no such thing, Mr. Linsley!"

"I'll break the door down if you don't, Hen. Come on, open up."

The door opens a crack and I see a sliver of Hen's face.

"Haven't you caused enough trouble, Mr. Linsley? What's the matter?"

"I need to speak to Mr. Wellesley-Clegg urgently."

"You can't, sir," she says through a mouthful of pins. "He left an hour ago."

"Left?"

"Yes, sir, for Lancashire. The house is falling down again, it seems."

"Hen," I say, "you must help me rescue Miss Wellesley-Clegg from that whoremonger."

"You mind your tongue, Mr. Linsley. She doesn't want to be rescued, so you leave her alone, the poor young lady."

"Hen, I beg of you—" The door shuts with a sharp click.

"Sir," says a voice behind me, "sir, I must go in there, if you please."

I step back and allow a traffic of women in and out of the room, and wander away, full of dismay. I must write a letter immediately to Mr. Wellesley-Clegg—while I could chase after him, that would leave Philomena unprotected, and I dare not risk it.

Even now that unspeakable false captain may be taking the sort of liberties with her with which I am only too familiar.

I return to the center of the house, where the main staircase, now adorned with the statue of Diana we bought together, holds sway. Behind me, people are involved in arriving, dealing with cloaks and fans and servants, and ahead of me, on the stairs, Beauty descends.

Alone, thank God.

She sees me and looks alarmed. One hand disappears behind her back, as though to hide what she carries—some sort of small bag, I think.

"Good evening, Mr. Linsley."

"What are you doing, Philomena?"

"Pray let me pass, sir."

"Is it true? That you are engaged to that man?"

"Yes." Does her lip tremble? "Please leave me alone."

"Philomena, I must speak to you. It is a matter of life or death. I beg of you, give me five minutes of your time."

"I have nothing to say to you, sir. Now let me pass."

"Please." I grasp her wrist.

She sighs and gives a quick look around. "Very well." She leads the way, not into the water-closet, to my relief, but into a small room that holds a few chairs and some cloaks.

"You cannot marry him, Philomena."

"Oh, well, if that is all . . ." She attempts to push past me.

"He is not what he seems. He is a fraud."

"How dare you!"

"The only thing he's captain of is Mrs. Bright's establishment. I met him there that night."

"You are despicable! Will you stoop to nothing to destroy my happiness?" She glares at me like a small, pretty terrier facing a rat. "He is a good and decent man. He is not rich, but he is noble and selfless. Why, do you know he spends his income on the unfortunate members of his regiment who have no pension? He—"

"Indeed. You believe he is out performing good works every night, I suppose? Love makes a fool of you. I'll wager he presses for an early marriage so he can lay his hands on your fortune the quicker—"

"Stop it, Inigo!"

"Please don't tell me you are giving him money." I reach behind her, momentarily distracted by her soft curves, and coins jingle as she attempts to evade me.

"I am. There is a dreadful case of a soldier with only one leg and six children to feed, and of course I said I should help. Now go away, Inigo. I never want to see you again."

"I'll tell your father. I intend to write to him directly. Are you stealing from your own family for this man?"

"Certainly not. Papa left it for me to do with as I wished."

She wriggles against me with distracting results. "If you don't let go of me I shall scream."

I release her. "Where is Blackwater?"

"I shall not tell you." She breaks away and runs out into the foyer, then beckons to a couple of footmen. They are large, serious-looking men, obviously hired for the occasion. They advance on me, with an obvious air of menace, despite the ridiculous Chinese costumes they wear.

"Now, sir," one says to me, "we hear you've had a bit too much to drink. Don't you think you'd best go home and leave the young ladies alone?"

They easily outweigh me together by ten stone at least. They thrust my cloak into my arms and me down the steps of the house with polite insistence.

I catch a hackney home to send an urgent letter to Mr. Wellesley-Clegg in Lancashire, and pray I am not too late. I swear to him that I will do anything to protect his daughter and that I love her beyond reason.

But I fear she is lost to me.

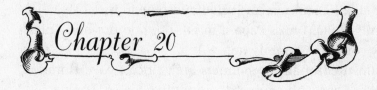

Chapter 20

Miss Philomena Wellesley-Clegg

I did not expect to be bored when I became an engaged woman, and I am ashamed to admit it.

Horatio is too busy with his poor soldiers to spend much time in society. I do wish he would let me accompany him, but when I asked, he took my hands and told me with great sweetness that he had to go into very low parts of London and did not wish me to be shocked. He calls every afternoon, and we have tête-à-têtes that, regretfully, my sisters never interrupt and I am almost used to his kisses now.

He does not dance because of a wound in his left leg. I believe it is his left leg. I thought I saw him limp on the right side one time, and he became a little annoyed at my concern and finally admitted that, yes, indeed, he had suffered a slight wound there also. He is too modest to talk much of his military exploits, and rarely wears his uniform, although he looks excessively handsome in it.

I miss Julia. I miss Papa. I miss—no, I do not miss Inigo. How could I? Certainly not.

I am tired of all my bonnets and, since I gave Horatio's soldiers Papa's fifty guineas, cannot in good conscience buy another on account. I spend fretful, lonely hours waiting for him to call each day. And it is only Tuesday, three days after my ball!

The Dowager Duchess called on Sunday, and again today, and she and Mama spend hours giggling together in her bedchamber, where she receives only her most favored friends. The twins report that they talk quite obscenely about female subjects, and I forbid them to listen at the keyhole anymore. This most recent time, however, they say, the Dowager Countess wept, and I cannot believe that. How absurd! Unless they were tears of joy at their reconciliation.

Oh, I am dreadfully out of sorts.

And Horatio has shown me a special license he carries, and begged me to make him the happiest of men. Why, my own papa almost suggested we should steal away and marry. Maybe I should. Occasionally, Hen nudges me and says I've been a maiden too long, and why don't I just take the captain and have done with it? I remind her we must wait until Papa has returned, for I am sure he would like to be present at my nuptials.

I look through the newspaper, hoping to improve myself, and see a report of the previous night's entertainment at Drury Lane. I wish I had been there, for it was a benefit performance for its star, Mrs. Frances Gibbons, and that probably implies it was her last appearance. But as I read on, I find that Mrs. Gibbons did not appear, the management claiming her indisposed, and the audience near rioted.

I lay the newspaper down and think about this. It is not like Mrs. Gibbons to turn down a performance, and I wonder if she is truly unwell. At any rate, the news means she may have left for the country already, and I am sorry I did not say good-bye to her, for I liked her very much.

I go in search of Hen, who is in the drawing room listening to Lydia and Charlotte play the piano as hideously as ever while she mends stockings.

"Hen, I have decided to pay a call on Miss Celia Blundell."

"I thought she was cutting you, miss, same as the Countess of Terrant."

"Well, no. I don't think so."

"Take her half a dozen cakes, miss, and you'll have her eating out of your hand." She looks with longing at the cosy fireplace. She has her shoes off and skirts rolled up and wears a faded, comfortable old gown.

"You don't have to come, Hen. You've been so busy with the ball and everything else, I think you should stay home and rest."

"I don't know what your mama would say." She jabs her needle into the stocking. "You be careful, now, miss."

I leave her droning on about sinners roiling in eternal flames in discordant counterpoint to Clementi, and the footman summons me a hackney to take me to the Blundells' house. Naturally, as soon as we have left I tell the driver to go instead to Soho, and soon we pull up at Mrs. Gibbons's little house. It is small and crooked, stuck in between two bigger ones like an afterthought, and I am glad to see the chimney smokes, so someone must be home.

I pay the driver and he pulls away. It strikes me then I should have asked him to wait, in case Mrs. Gibbons has decided to cut me too, but it is too late, and I ring the door-bell.

The door flies open almost immediately.

Inigo stands there.

My first thought is how very debauched he looks—he is unshaven, is in his shirt-sleeves, and his feet are bare. I have never seen a man's bare feet before, a gentleman's, that is, and he has very long, elegant toes with black hair on them. And his shirt placket is unbuttoned, as though he has just pulled it over his head, and I can see a smudge of similar hair there too.

And then I am horrified and hurt. He has gone back to Mrs. Gibbons's bed, and has just risen from it, by his looks.

He leans against the doorframe, with no pretence at a bow. "Go away, Philomena."

From inside the house comes a high, continuous wail.

Fanny appears. She looks little better than Inigo, wearing a loose wrapper, with her hair uncombed, eyes red and swollen, and she clutches a large bundle against her chest. It is this bundle that makes the wretched wailing sound.

"Inigo, is it—oh. Miss Wellesley-Clegg, it's kind of you to call, but I cannot receive visitors. I'm sorry. Please go."

"What's happened?" I ask. I push past Inigo and Fanny turns back the shawl around Will.

What I see shocks me. The plump, laughing baby I remember has wasted away, his skin waxen, and I can see the shape of his skull beneath his face. He opens his mouth and cries feebly. When I touch his skin it is hot and dry.

"I thought you were the doctor," Inigo says, stepping back inside the house. "You must go. This is no place for you."

"What happened?" I whisper again, horrified.

"He's been ill for two days. He . . ." Inigo rests his head against the wall, and raises one hand to his face. His shoulders shake. He's crying, and this horrifies me even more.

I look at the two exhausted people, and the poor child they are trying to keep alive, and shut the door. "Let me help you."

Tears run down Fanny's face. She shakes her head and murmurs something about how it would not be proper, but leads the way into the house. It is a dreadful mess, belongings packed into wooden crates, and then half-unpacked, and sawdust from them spilling onto the floor.

I've said I will help them, but in truth I don't know what I can do. I don't know what anyone can do with a child as sick as this.

"I sent Molly to make tea a half hour ago," Fanny says. She sinks onto a sofa half-covered with gowns.

Will wails again.

"Let me take him." Inigo, his face smeared, takes his son. He begins to shamble up and down the room, in a way that suggests he has spent many hours so.

I go to find the kitchen, down a narrow flight of stairs. A girl of about thirteen slumps over the kitchen table, fast asleep, while a kettle boils dry on the fire. I don't have the heart to wake her. I find a shawl that I spread over her and turn to deal with the kettle. I almost burn myself before bringing my petticoat into use, and take the kettle to the stone sink, where I pump more water into it.

When I've put the kettle back on the fire, I turn my attention to a pile of dishes in the sink. I could take more from the half-packed crate under the table, but consider this would only make more mess. I scrub cups and saucers as best I can with a vile yellow soap that smells of farmyards and leaves my hands red and raw.

I am not a total fool around the kitchen, but my experience has been making pastry and other delicacies, and someone else, like this skinny child with her reddened hands, scrubs the pots after I've finished. I have always been surrounded by deferential servants who take care I do not burn myself or work too hard.

I add a little more coal to the fire, and, later rather than sooner, find an apron to wear. I am quite filthy. I wonder if they have medicine for Will, or whether we should give him some boiled water, or milk.

I find the milk in a jug in a large crock, and it smells quite sweet. Not so the butter, greasy and with a fly struggling in it. There is a loaf of bread I hack apart—I did not realize it was so hard to slice bread thinly—and spread with marmalade. I suspect neither Inigo nor Fanny have eaten much while their child is sick. There is little food in the house, and I think it likely Fanny orders from one of the cookhouses on the street.

And all the while, above my head, Will cries and cries, and Inigo's feet pace up and down.

Mr. Inigo Linsley

I did not think I would ever smile again, not after these two days and nights willing my son to live.

But the sight of Miss Philomena Wellesley-Clegg, with a black smear of coal on her round face, carrying a tea tray and a kettle of boiling water does that. Her hair has gone into spirals in the kitchen heat, she has tucked her skirts up into the apron ties to manage the stairs, and beams with pride at her accomplishment. She finds the tea caddy and makes tea, pausing to polish the cups and spoons clean on her apron. "I didn't wash them very well," she says. "I think I should have used hot water. Shall I take Will, Inigo?"

I can't bear to let someone else hold him, tortured as I am by his cries and my powerlessness to help him, but I hand him over. She tries to not let me see the horror on her face, at how hot and insubstantial he feels, and at that moment I love her more than anything in the world—except Will.

Fanny and I are both dazed and half-mad from lack of sleep and worry, and Philomena, I think, senses this. She does not try to talk to us, or ask about Will's condition, which is all too obvious. She pours some water into a saucer, and I show her how we try to feed Will with a teaspoon. He barely has the strength now to swallow, and we offer him drops on our fingers as though he were a kitten. Fanny has tried to get him to take her breast for two days, and he turns his head aside and cries, too feeble to suck.

When the doorbell rings, Philomena hands Will to me, and goes to answer it.

"Inigo, do not threaten to kill this one," Fanny says.

The doctor comes into the drawing room, with Philomena behind him. From the look on her face she has never before had a jumped-up tradesman enter a room in front of her, and clutches his hat, gloves and bag with a helpless look on her face.

Dr. Silver, recommended by the baker a few doors down, is quite different from the other savages who have seen Will in the last few days. He is thin and dark, and speaks with a foreign accent.

Philomena stares at him with great interest, and I realize she has probably never seen a Jew before. He catches her gaze, and smiles. "Ah, your maid is not clever, I think? But a good girl, I can tell."

He examines Will with great gentleness, and asks us how long our child has been ill, the usual questions, and then covers him up again. "You must make him drink. Keep him warm. Let him take the breast if he will."

"That's all?" If I were not so tired I would throttle this so-called man of science. He is as great a charlatan as the others, if not more so, for this is what we have done for over two days, and watched Will fade from us.

"Sir, if you wish to have your child bled or purged, there are plenty in my profession who will oblige you, but I think he suffers enough."

"Inigo, do not bully him," Fanny says. We are both aware of what I have threatened to do to the other doctors who have wanted to inflict these treatments, or worse, on my poor child.

"Yes, but, devil take it, surely there's something that can

be done?" I have been hoping for some magic potion, a miracle, and I see now none is forthcoming.

"You may bathe him in warm water, but do not let him get chilled. And pray, sir. It will not be too long, I think." His words could have sounded harsh, but from this man they have a certain comfort.

Fanny weeps, hunched up on the sofa, holding Will again at her bare breast. His head rolls away from her.

Dr. Silver stops in front of Philomena and she releases his hat and gloves. "Look after your master and mistress," he says with a kindly smile. "They should eat and rest."

"Yes, sir. I made them tea, sir, all on my own, but I did not wash the dishes very well."

"Very good." He pats her on the head and waits for her to open the door for him, which eventually she does. He gives us a smile as he leaves, apparently in appreciation of how good we are to take on this simpleton as our maid. I wonder if we shall ever be able to laugh about this together.

Philomena, her voice muffled, announces she is going downstairs, and I suspect she is going to cry where she will not distress us. I hear some banging about, and the sound of a plate or some such breaking. Fanny and I take turns walking up and down with our son in our arms, feeding drops of water in his mouth, and I am not sure if she prays, but I know I do.

After a while Molly comes upstairs, yawning and ashamed that she has slept, but not particularly surprised at the presence of an inept maid in her kitchen. Like me and Fanny, she is too tired to take in much. Miss Wellesley-Clegg has taken it upon herself to go to the cookshop, it appears, and charged Molly with bringing up water in which to bathe our son.

Philomena comes in, rather pink about the face, with a large pie, and I realize the unseemliness of a gently-bred woman going on such an errand. I ask her if she is all right.

"Oh, yes," she says, a little too brightly. "Some of the gentlemen in the street commented on my—my ankles, and one of them said I was a plump chicken ready for plucking. At least, I think that is what he said."

Her ankles, with her skirts still tucked up to negotiate the stairs, are indeed on display, and I wish I could appreciate them more. "Philomena, you must go home. Please. This is not a proper place for you to be. I am exceedingly grateful, but you should not be here. It's getting late. Please, my love."

She looks at me oddly. "Don't be a ninny, Inigo. Besides, I have sent word home that I am with a sick friend, so do not worry about it. Now, you must eat."

She bathes Will while Fanny and I pick at the food, and then we light the lamps and settle in for another night.

After we have eaten, Philomena and Molly go downstairs into the kitchen, and I hear a loud scream. Philomena, skirts held up to her knees, rushes back upstairs. "Huge black beetles!" she announces. "Oh, I'm sorry, but I cannot go down there."

"It's all right, miss," Molly calls up the stairs. "You get used to them. They won't hurt you."

"I'll go down in the morning," Philomena says, "Molly says they don't come out in daylight. But, if I may, I'll stay up here."

"Philomena, dearest," Fanny says, "we did not intend to banish you to the kitchen. And you're sure you won't go home?"

"Not if you want me to stay."

"I am so grateful . . ." Fanny breaks down in Philomena's arms, weeping as though her heart is broken, which indeed I think it is.

Chapter 21

Miss Philomena Wellesley-Clegg

It is a dreadful night. We take it in turns, myself, Fanny, Inigo, and Molly, in walking up and down with Will. He has a cradle that gives him the continual movement he craves, but seems greatly distressed if he is placed there. Inigo tries to persuade Fanny to sleep, and she him, but neither can. Both of them are now so tired they will fall asleep if they sit, and then come awake, roused by their own fear.

And to think they have borne this for two nights already. Church bells chime the quarters, and time becomes distorted—sometimes it is as though a whole night passes between the chimes, and other times only seconds seem to have passed.

I send Molly to bed at midnight. She sleeps among the black beetles, which horrifies me, but she assures me it is what she is used to.

And gradually there is a change in Will's condition. He drinks a little more water, and then cries for more. When we bathe him his eyes open and he gazes at Fanny, with his poor little chapped lips turning up in a smile. He even nurses for a few minutes, before falling asleep, his skin finally cooled down, and it may be my fancy, but he begins to look more like a living child.

When four o'clock strikes, the four of us stagger into Fanny's bedchamber, I carrying a cup of water and a spoon in case Will wishes to drink more, and Fanny and Inigo swaying like a pair of drunks. Fanny sinks onto the bed with her child and falls asleep immediately.

"Inigo," I say, and I blush like a rising sun, and am glad it is still dark, "this is most improper, and I am so sorry to ask you, but could you unlace my stays? I should like to lie down on the sofa for a little."

He laughs and unfastens my gown and then my stays with a startling deftness that suggests he has had some experience with women's clothing. "Stay here. I'll keep you warm."

And he does. He encircles me in his arms and I lie against him and try to stay awake to savor the wondrousness of this moment—his scent (somewhat sweaty and smoky from being inside for so long, but still delicious), the slow, steady beat of his heart, the mystery of male sinew and muscle and bone. But I can't. I am too tired and too content to do anything but fall asleep.

When I awake it is almost light, and I am struck by the

extreme impropriety of what has just occurred. I am glad I did not realize it at the time, but Inigo has dispensed with his trousers and wears only his shirt and a pair of cotton underdrawers, something I find fascinating in a dreadful kind of seventeen shillings and sixpence way (if I still maintained the fund). Worse still, his arm is draped across me, and his hand is right inside my shift.

It has nothing to do with milking cows. Nothing at all.

"What's wrong?" he mumbles and pulls me closer. He lifts my hand to his lips and kisses the burns I suffered during my brief stint as housemaid.

"Inigo, I have to go home."

"No, you don't. Not yet." He rolls away from me, to my relief, and looks at his son.

Will has extricated one of his mother's breasts and sucks away with great energy.

Inigo cups his son's head for a moment, and then turns back to me. "Please don't marry Blackwater. Even if I'm entirely wrong about him, which I assure you I'm not, you can't marry him."

"But I promised I would. My mama and papa expect it. Everyone does. Besides, are you sure you are not mistaken? You were rather foxed that night."

"Not that foxed. I love you, Philomena. Marry me."

"Inigo, this is most irregular. We are in bed with your mistress and your natural son and you cannot propose here."

"Oh yes he can, and he should. Accept him, Philomena." Fanny is awake now. She frowns and scratches her mop of hair. "Will is wet. I'd best see to him."

"I'll take him." I struggle into my gown, pick Will up, and kiss his cheek. I can hear Molly banging around in the kitchen and consider it probably safe from black beetles now.

Inigo follows me.

"Sir, pray put on your nether garments!" I rush out of the room with Will damp and cooing in my arms.

"Philomena"—he is trying to button his trousers and negotiate the stairs behind me, and I fear we shall all fall down—"if you wish to be honorable, then pray break off the engagement before accepting me. I'll get a special license—ah, there's my boy, what a fine big c—k he has indeed."

"Oh, do have some propriety, Inigo." I look up from the kitchen table, where his son grasps his appendage and laughs as though he has never been at death's door. That, I suppose, says much about men in general. "I promise, I'll speak to Hor—Blackwater. I'll talk to Mama, and Papa too when he comes back. How can I make a promise to you when I'm promised to another? What would your family think?"

"Oh, the devil take my family," he says as I fight to swathe the wriggly baby in cotton. I finally leave Will in Molly's more capable hands.

I rush around the house collecting my shoes, pelisse, gloves and bonnet. My stays are discarded on the floor and I roll them up tightly under one arm, hoping no one will guess what I carry. Without them I feel most peculiar, and my dress looks like a sack, but I will not ask Inigo to lace me into them. It would be dreadfully improper.

Inigo follows, generally getting in the way, and puts his own coat, stockings and boots on. "I can at least summon you a hackney," he says. "You're sure I can't escort you home?"

I know he is torn between leaving his son and accompanying me, and I tell him to stay with Fanny and Will. I shall have to make a discreet entrance into our house, and I certainly do not want to arrive home with a debauched-looking gentleman as my escort.

When I get back to the house I enter through the servants' quarters, hoping I will not see any black beetles. What I do see is Hen, with curling papers in her hair, and some of the other staff having breakfast. They stare at me, and then their chairs scrape back as they rise.

"It's all right. Please don't get up." My hands are suddenly weak and clumsy, and to my shame, I burst into tears as my stays tumble onto the floor. I know I cry from relief and exhaustion, but heaven only knows what they think.

"It's all right, miss." Hen scoops up my stays and guides me upstairs, murmuring of hot baths and breakfast while I weep uncontrollably.

I fall asleep before my bathwater is brought, and then fall asleep in it. Hen puts salve on my burns, tut-tuts at the state of my gown, but asks no questions. She feeds me tea and toast before I tumble gratefully into my warm bed and sleep again.

"Miss Philomena, Miss Philomena! You must wake up!"

I struggle out of a deep sleep, where I have been wandering through dim passages trying to find a crying baby. "Hen, what's the matter?"

"The captain's here, miss."

"But it's only ten o'clock. What does he want?" I am quite stupid with sleep. Meanwhile, Hen bustles around the room, pulling out finery.

"You know what he wants, miss. Up with you, now."

And then my mother rushes into the room, and there is no peace. "Come why are you in bed still I hope Miss

Blundell is well now it is a pity you came home so late for she could be a bridesmaid but Lydia and Charlotte will suffice I think the ball gown with the long sleeves from the merino Hen my the Captain is in a great hurry he swears he will have you today before he dies of love—"

"Mama! Mama!" I run to her. "You mean the captain wants to marry me today?"

"Indeed yes it is as you arranged why you cunning vixen he told us how you meant to run off with him and I was so grateful he was more mindful of your reputation than you were miss I should be angry but love is a wondrous thing indeed and he is so tall and handsome—"

"I will not marry him!" I roar in the voice I usually reserve for Charlotte and Lydia. "Tell him to go away! I never arranged to elope with him. It is a wicked lie. I don't love him!"

"Too late, miss," Hen says. "He's downstairs claiming he'll throw himself in the Thames if you do not take him."

"Let him!" I dash to the window and fling it open in the hopes that Inigo waits below on a white charger, but there is instead a man with a dancing dog playing a fiddle, that is the man plays the fiddle, not the dog. "Help!" I shriek before Hen pulls me away.

"Now, miss, everything will be all right. Don't you worry—"

"Vile deceiver!" I say to Hen as though I were one of Fanny's tragic heroines and scream loudly again. I regret to say there is something quite enjoyable in all of this. "Papa didn't mean this to happen. I will not marry him! I never made him any such promise!"

"Miss," Hen hisses into my ear, "you're engaged to him,

and if that's not a promise to marry, what is? Besides, if you do not marry him you'll be ruined after last night, and your sisters with you. Shame on you!"

Loud, booted male feet clump up the stairs. "Where is she, ma'am?"

"—oh pray sir this is most irregular you cannot come in here why see how she blushes oh Philly my dear cover yourself oh and here are my two youngest all dressed and ready to be bridesmaids my dears you do look well Lydia do you wear the yellow ribbon it is no matter although what I shall do when Philly is gone to tell you apart I do not know—"

"Get out!" I scream to the room in general and hurl a certain china receptacle in the direction of the doorway. I regret it is not empty.

The captain swears mightily and retreats, as do all the others. I rush to lock the door, then scramble up onto the bed, wrap my arms around a bedpost, and burst into tears of humiliation.

Outside there is a whispered conversation I cannot hear properly, and then blessed silence.

After a while, there is a timid knock on the door. "Philly, may I come in?"

"Which one of you is it?" Even I can't tell from their voices.

"Charlotte, sister."

"Are you alone?"

A giggle and a scuffle. "Yes."

I open the door and call down the passage, "Lydia—no, Charlotte—you shall not listen at the door. Go away."

Lydia, for it is she, comes into the room. She carries a glass that she holds out to me.

"Is he still here?" I ask.

"Yes. They took his coat downstairs for the servants to clean. What shall you do, Philly?"

"I don't know." I sniff the contents of the glass. "What is this?"

"Brandy. We thought it might do you good. You look unwell."

"Thank you." Kindness from even one of my horrid younger sisters is welcome at this moment. I cannot get over the captain's perfidy—as though I would elope with him! On the other hand, I cannot distinctly remember telling him the engagement is off, although I think throwing a chamberpot at the gentleman in question could be interpreted as such.

"I am so tired, Lyddie." I take a sip of the brandy. It tastes quite unpleasant, and burns my mouth.

"Hen put valerian in to calm you," Lydia says.

The serving of brandy is large and takes me some time to drink, and I feel bone weary by the time I have finished. "I can't move," I tell my sister. "Let me sleep a little."

I have some very peculiar dreams after that. Mama and Hen come to see me, and help me dress. I am like a rag doll, and giggle as I flop around. We go outside the house briefly, and then ride in a carriage, and I find myself in a large, echoing place with high pillars, clinging to a gentleman's arm.

A lot of familiar people are there, members of the *ton*, and it is rather like one of those dreams where you find yourself at Almack's in your shift. But I do not wear my shift. I am wearing the gown I wore at the ball with hastily stitched-in long sleeves, and a gentleman in black asks me questions.

I can hear people rustling behind me, and I turn to see Papa, which of course is absurd, as he is in Lancashire where our house is falling down.

The kindly gentleman in the black robe asks me a very silly question—if I want to take this man as my husband—and I turn to see the captain beside me. His hand is under my arm and he frowns at me. He looks a little apprehensive—he is chewing his lip, and he gives me a shake.

Oh. I am supposed to answer the question. Do I want to take this man as my lawful wedded husband?

Well, of course not. How absurd. This is only a dream, so I can say whatever I want to.

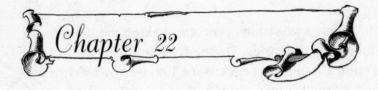

Chapter 22

Mr. Inigo Linsley

I am so deeply in love that after seeing my sweet girl into a hackney, I fall asleep, although not immediately. I stay in the kitchen with Molly and Will and watch my son devour bread dipped in milk, take him upstairs and let him crawl around the floor for a little, and applaud him mightily when he belches. After a while he becomes fretful and yawns, and falls asleep in my arms. I take him upstairs to his mother, and then lie on the sofa. Only for a little, I promise myself. I shall not sleep. I couldn't sleep a wink last night, or this morning, or whenever it was we retired, not after that delicious invitation to remove Miss Wellesley-Clegg's stays. Nor after holding her while she snuggled against me, as trusting and sweet as a kitten, with her hair tickling my face.

And she has agreed to get rid of that pimp and marry me!

I am rudely awoken by someone shaking me.

"Wake up, Mr. Linsley. There's trouble."

"Trouble?" I open my eyes to see Tom Darrowby with one half of a familiar pair, a twin, that is. "Miss Charlotte or Miss Lydia? What are you doing here?" I struggle to my feet. "And which one are you?"

"Oh, sir, I have poisoned my sister!"

"What?"

She continues to stare at me while Darrowby, behind her, mouths something at me.

Trousers.

I grab my nether garments (as Miss Wellesley-Clegg refers to them) and put them on. "What the devil do you mean, Miss Charlotte or Miss Lydia?"

"I am Lydia. I gave her laudanum, sir, for she was much agitated. I decided to double the dose, so she would fall asleep, like Juliet in *Romeo and Juliet*, and then . . ."

". . . And then I could visit the family tomb? You ninny, Miss Lydia. Where is she?"

"Gone to the church with the captain."

I say a few words that I'm fairly sure Miss Lydia has not heard before while grabbing my coat and boots.

"Miss Lydia came to our house to find me. The fact of the matter is, Philomena will agree to anything while she's drunk as a lord on opiate," Darrowby says as he hurries us downstairs and we scramble into a hackney. "Mr. and Mrs.

Pullen attend a christening in the church, and I asked them to try and delay matters as long as they could. The captain has a special license and I'm afraid she'll marry him before she knows what she does."

I lean out of the window and shout to the driver, "A guinea for you if you can get us to St. George's in ten minutes." I turn to my companions. "Does either of you have a guinea?"

We careen through the streets, weaving in and out of traffic, and causing some horrible tangles at crossroads.

"I don't want her to marry the captain," Lydia says, as the driver of a cartful of wine casks enlarges her vocabulary a little more.

"Has your papa said something of him?"

"No. It is that the captain looks at our bosoms and not at our faces when he talks to us."

Given the twins' skinny frames, that must be decidedly unrewarding for him.

"Scoundrel," growls Darrowby as we take a corner so fast we nearly overturn.

"How the devil did you know where to find me, Darrowby?"

He looks at me with great disapproval. "I was Fan—Mrs. Gibbons's guest the night you . . . when you came to call somewhat the worse for drink. Since you were not with your family at the church, I thought Mrs. Gibbons's house the best place to seek you out."

It's my turn to look at him with disapproval. I only just stop myself from asking him if his intentions toward Fanny are honorable, as if I were her brother and not her protector.

As we pull up in Hanover Square, I leap out, narrowly

avoiding a nursemaid who carries a squalling bundle of antique lace down the steps. Once inside the church, I find the cream of the *ton* has lingered to see an impromptu wedding, my family among them. And I fear I'm too late.

Philomena, swaying slightly, stands with the captain before the minister. The captain, his fine profile presented to the assembled, glares at her.

"Oh, no," she says. "I really don't like the way he kisses."

The minister, who appears nonplussed by an answer not covered by the prayerbook of the Church of England, recoils. He asks her, with a touch of panic in his voice, if she will take this man to be her lawful wedded husband.

She giggles. "Don't be absurd."

"She means she will," says the captain. "Pray continue."

"She may do so, sir, but she must say the words."

Philomena smiles happily at us all. "You see, I don't love him. I thought I did, but I don't. I love someone else, and I went to bed with him last night, and it was so very pleasant I don't think I want to go to bed with anyone else, ever. Particularly you, Horatio." She lowers her gaze to a part of a gentleman a lady rarely looks at directly, and adds, "Twopence ha'penny."

Terrant approaches me and grips my arm. "Good God, Inigo, what have you done? I presume it was you?"

Philomena meanwhile begins to weave drunkenly down the aisle, still talking. "Isn't it strange how everyone is here? Lady Blundell, you really shouldn't wear that color, it looks hideous on you, and Celia, you stole that way of trimming your bonnet from me, but I forgive you. Papa, aren't you supposed to be in Lancashire? Oh, Aylesworth, that is a splendid waistcoat, and I am so glad you and the Mad Poet are such good friends, it is quite charming . . ."

Terrant grips my arm in a hold like iron. "Don't go near her!"

"Let me go. I must rescue her—"

But Lady Rowbotham steps forward and intercepts Philomena. "You come along with me, my dear, and you won't have to deal with any of these unpleasant males."

"Thank God," Terrant says, still holding on to me as though he were press-ganging me. "I thought for one moment you were about to disgrace our family."

"But she—I—"

"I forbid you to go near her."

"You forbid me? Who the devil do you think you are, to talk to me so?"

He hisses in my ear, "I am the head of this family, something you have seem to forgotten, and I will not have you make an alliance with a woman who has spoken so, and in public. She is from Trade and nothing but a common—"

I struggle in his grip before kicking his shin and he releases me. At this point, still half-crazed with lack of sleep and horror at what Philomena has done, I think I go a little mad. I forget my brother is the Earl of Terrant. Instead, all the childish quarrels and fights (which I usually lost) of the past two decades crowd into my mind, and within seconds we are rolling on the church floor, trying to beat each other to a pulp.

A deluge of cold water brings us to our senses before either of us can do too much damage to the other.

Our mother stands over us, the silver jug used in baptisms

in her hand. "I have never been so ashamed in my life!"

We stand and shuffle our feet like the stupid schoolboys we seem to have become again.

"I am only glad your father was not alive to see this. We shall go home now, where you may both reflect on your behavior. Terrant, you shall call a family meeting."

"Yes, Mama," we chorus, damp and dispirited, the devils cast out of us by the holy water and our mother's disapproval. We slink out of the church, while a chorus of spiteful gossip arises behind us.

After an unhappy, silent ride home, we gather in Pudgebum's study and glower at each other. Julia cries. I suppose it is her condition. My mother, to my surprise, holds her hand.

"It's your choice," Pudgebum says. "Marry her if you must, but you'll not see any of us again. I can't take Weaselcopse from you, but it should provide an adequate, if modest, income. However, there is also this matter, which I think may make you consider your situation rather carefully."

He produces a piece of paper.

"By God, you opened a letter to me!"

I make a grab for it, but he whisks it away. For one moment, I think it might be a letter from Philomena, and he intends to read it aloud, but when he does so, it is far worse, and far more shameful.

"It is not a letter, Inigo. It is a bill. Item: Services of a lady of the house, two hundred guineas, with additional surcharge of fifty guineas per person, total three hundred and fifty guineas."

Good God.

"Inigo," Julia says, "tell him—"

I assume a frosty demeanor similar to my brother's and frown at her. "This is none of your business, madam. Women have no right to involve themselves in gentlemen's affairs. It is most indelicate, and frankly, madam, I am surprised you put yourself forward so." I am damned if Julia will implicate herself and be subjected to Terrant's bullying.

He continues, "Item: Supper for five at ten guineas per person, fifty guineas."

I open my mouth to protest that only one of our party actually ate anything—and lost it again shortly after—before realizing I will only get myself and others into deeper water by speaking.

"Item: Damage to carpet, ten guineas."

I'm not even aware what this is for, so can only guess it had something to do with the unfortunate lobster episode.

"Item: Five bottles champagne at five guineas apiece, twenty-five guineas." Terrant glares at me. "Less a deposit of thirty-two guineas, with a balance of three hundred and thirty-three guineas remaining. And exactly how do you intend to pay for this, brother? Even if you marry Miss Wellesley-Clegg I doubt her family will allow her that extravagant dowry after her exposure today. If they have any decency at all they will cut her off without a shilling."

I open my mouth to mention my next quarter's allowance, until I realize there will be no allowance, only my very modest rents from Weaselcopse. I am heavily in Queer Street now, no mistake. So I say nothing.

"So, I think that concludes the matter." He looks extremely pleased with himself. "However, there is one more item to discuss."

He means this could be worse? I brace myself.

But to my surprise, Pudgebum addresses our mother. "I see that other military gentleman who so recently graced us with his presence, Admiral Riley, has not visited our house recently."

"Indeed." My mother glares back at him.

"There has been some talk, madam."

My mother sets Julia aside with a gentle pat on her shoulder and stands to face her oldest son, the head of our family. I stand also, but to my horror, Pudgebum remains seated. My mother notices it too, and flushes at his blatant insult.

He continues, "You are his mistress."

What? My mother?

She shrugs, and looks down her nose at him. "Indeed, sir."

Pudgebum stands then, realizing she looks down on him, and it gives him little advantage. "You dishonor the family, madam."

She says nothing.

He leans forward, hands spread on his desk. "I must request you leave for the country immediately. I cannot have our family name dragged further into the mud. I have written to request the dower house at Inchcombe be made ready for you."

"Inchcombe?" I am outraged. It's the furthest property from London and our other lands in Buckinghamshire, little more than a farmhouse surrounded by desolate grazing grounds, and the dower house is damp and gloomy. "Terrant, that is not just. Our mother—"

"I am head of the family, Inigo, and I make the decisions. You will stay there until I see fit, madam. I regret I can allow you no contact with the family."

She knows what this means—we all do. She will be denied the pleasure of welcoming her next grandchild into the world until Terrant relents. My mother curtsies, and sweeps from the room, head held high, and for a brief moment, Terrant looks uncomfortable.

I break the uneasy silence that falls after she has gone. "You swine," I say to my brother. "You appalling, dishonorable, unkind swine."

And I follow my mother out of the room.

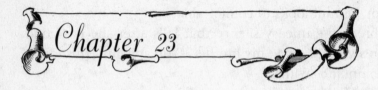

Chapter 23

Mr. Inigo Linsley

My mother sits at her writing desk, picking through a box of jewels and letters as I enter her bedchamber. Normally I would not dare invade her privacy in such a way, but I am too incensed to care.

She says nothing as I enter the room but raises one eyebrow in a way calculated to strike fear into lesser beings.

"It's abominable," I bluster. "That he should insult you so. To suggest such a thing, that you . . . that you . . ."

The look in her eyes, ironic and cynical, makes me blunder to a stop.

Not my mother. Surely not.

With Sev. With *anyone*.

My good intentions flee, and I bellow, in a pale imitation of my brother, "Good God, have you no shame? At your age?"

"Oh, for God's sake, not you too! It's bad enough that Terrant lectures me as though he were a mealy-mouthed parson!" She stands and fairly shouts at me. "I am seven-and-forty, Inigo. I have been alone for six years. I know you think I am a monster, but I was once beautiful and am still considered handsome, and I have, how many more years to live? A good forty, if my family are anything to go by."

This is true. I have a vast collection of troublesome great-aunts and uncles, and my great-grandfather and great-grandmother on her side of the family still live.

She continues, "I have always done my duty. Always. I was a virtuous wife. I turned a blind eye to your father's infidelities because I loved him, and . . ."

I wish I had not heard that. It is little more than I always suspected, for we are of the *ton*, and this is how things so often are.

". . . And now, when I find I wanted something more in my life than being the respectable Dowager Countess—"

"And you've certainly achieved that, madam. I don't think anyone could call you respectable, now."

She growls and deals me a box on the ear that nearly fells me.

"Yes, with a whoremonger for a son, and a pompous fool for another!" She considers for a moment, and then adds, "And I think George's sermons are dreadful."

That undoes me. I collapse onto her bed and sit there rubbing my ear, helpless with laughter.

She glares at me. "I don't believe I gave you permission to sit."

"I beg your pardon." Well trained as ever by her, I leap to my feet. "I—I suppose there is no chance of marriage between you?"

"He asked for my hand."

Oh, thank God.

She continues, "And I told him I liked going to bed with him, but I didn't want to marry him. And I have not seen him since."

"Well, for God's sake, why won't you marry him? It will get you out from under Terrant's thumb, at least. I'll pay a call on Sev and—"

"Absolutely not! I will not be demeaned so." And then to my horror she bursts into tears and weeps without restraint, sinking back down into her chair with her elbows among her scattered jewels.

I'm horrified. I believe she wept when my sister died—at least, she locked herself into her bedchamber and emerged fierce and red-eyed a week later. And I remember the dreadful stillness that descended on her at my father's death—but I have never seen her like this before.

"Ma?" I haven't called her that in years. I touch her shoulder, fully expecting her to turn and snap at me.

She does. "Pray do not address me as though I were a housemaid and you my son!"

"I beg your pardon."

She buries her face in her hands. "Please leave me."

"No, Ma, I won't." I push a handkerchief against her fingers, and to my relief she takes it, but continues to cry.

I really don't understand women. She thinks it would be demeaning to marry the man she loves, purely because a third party intervenes on her behalf and gives him the answer she should have given in the first place? And this, after her humiliation at my brother's hands?

"You can't go to Inchcombe, Ma. It's unhealthy and you'll be lonely. Come to Weaselcopse with me."

She gives a small smile. "You know we would drive each other mad, Inigo, although it is very kind of you to offer. Besides, Terrant would never allow it."

"He doesn't have to know."

She sighs and picks through her jewels, pulling out a brooch and handing it to me. "Take this. They're diamonds, and you should be able to pay your debts, although I am greatly shamed that you should squander money on whores."

I look at the diamond brooch in my hands, the initials E and H twined together within a heart. My parents' initials. "I can't take this, Ma. It was a gift from Papa."

"Take it." She folds my hand over it. "I'm quite sure he wouldn't approve of what you have done—I certainly do not—but I think you have lost quite enough already." She lowers her eyes, and adds, "I wanted to thank you for your discretion, also."

"My discretion?"

"Yes. When you gave my busk to Julia's maid and she brought it to me."

"*Your* busk?" Now I'm outraged again. To think of my mother and her lover creeping off to do—well, actually the sort of thing I'd liked to have done with Philomena, if I were honest. The sort of thing I almost did with Lady Caroline Bludge while poor Philomena was in the room. "You mean—oh, good God. I—"

"Hold your tongue." She gives me a cynical look. "You finance orgies in whorehouses and intend to set up house with your mistress—"

"Former mistress, madam—"

She snorts. "Your mistress and your bastard, and you dare preach to me? You're almost as bad as Terrant, nay, worse, for he hardly has a brain in his head . . . why, Inigo, what's the matter?"

"Will almost died," I gasp and take my handkerchief back. "My son, Will. He was so ill, but he got better, and Philomena was there, too . . ."

"Oh, Inigo." She puts her arms around me, something she hasn't done in years. "Inigo, if—if I come to Weaselcopse, may I meet your son?"

"I'd be honored." I blow my nose, embarrassed now at my behavior, and step away from her.

"Of course, I couldn't possibly receive his mother."

"Of course not." I try to keep a straight face. "Heaven forfend."

She gives me her usual sort of look. "And the garden was a disgrace last time I visited."

We are back to normal, I believe, to our mutual relief. I cannot believe I have just invited this dreadful woman to share my country exile, and what is worse, to my horror she has accepted. I shall have to assign her rooms as far away from me as possible in the house, I shall have to creep out at night to plant weeds to occupy her in the daytime . . .

"Inigo?"

"Yes, madam?"

"You weren't listening, as usual. I asked you, what are you going to do about Philomena?"

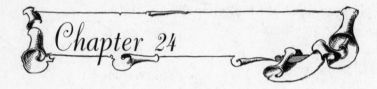

Chapter 24

Miss Philomena Wellesley-Clegg

When I come to my senses, I discover I was not dreaming. Before Aunt Rowbotham can whisk away the newspaper, I read a scurrilous cartoon, a rude poem, and a commentary by a lady of society on a certain vulgar display by a Miss W—C—. Worse, there is a letter from one of *those* Wellesleys, stating their commitment to upholding the flower of English maidenhood, full of vehement attacks upon those from Trade and those who seek to better their station by mixing with the *ton*.

Small memories of the previous day leak into my mind. Oh, I have ruined myself. I shall have to be a governess in some desolate mansion that is probably haunted and has brigands lurking in the dense forests surrounding it. I shall never see Inigo again or fall in love with anyone else. I may never see my mama and papa again—I cannot forget the shocked look on their faces, and Mama's complete and unnerving silence.

I spend much of that day crying and feeling quite ill from the opiate I took.

Aunt Rowbotham is herself, which is to say she forces me to give her pug Roland a bath, and then read aloud to her. The two of them snore and snort after dinner as I read from a book of improving sermons, occasionally pausing to wipe an errant tear.

She turns away all callers that day. The front doorbell rings frequently, and I am dying of curiosity to know who has called. Late in the afternoon, aunt Rowbotham summons me into the drawing room, where, to my surprise, Aylesworth and the Mad Poet rise from the sofa and bow.

"I don't hold with men," my aunt says, "but these two are harmless enough, Philomena. In fact, they hardly count. Roland, you will accompany me."

The pug waddles away behind her, tongue lolling, and leaving a strong odor of dog in his wake as they leave the room.

"What a vile creature," Aylesworth says, raising his handkerchief to his nose. "I mean the pug, of course. Well, Miss Wellesley-Clegg, I must congratulate you on your new reputation as the Jezebel of the *ton*."

"Oh, dear. Wasn't she the one who hammered a stake through someone's head?"

"Something of the sort." He eyes me critically. "You will ruin your complexion as well as your reputation if you insist on crying all day, my dear. Carrotte, give her your handkerchief and fetch her a glass of wine. That's better. Now, my dear Miss Wellesley-Clegg, I have a proposition for you."

Oh, heavens! He is about to ask me to become his mistress! I try to assume an expression of wounded virtue.

But why has he brought the Mad Poet with him? The Mad Poet, I see, is uncharacteristically silent, and gazes at him as though I were not in the room.

"I have a mother," Aylesworth says.

Well, everyone does, and I wonder why he has to point this out to me.

"D—d dreadful woman, if you'll pardon the expression, Miss Wellesley-Clegg. Makes Lady Rowbotham and the Dowager Countess of Terrant look like angels. She's insistent and meddling. Tends to burst in upon a fellow's bedchamber at the most awkward of moments."

I take a sip of wine and nod encouragingly, wondering why he shares his family reminiscences with me.

The Mad Poet, I notice, lays a hand on Aylesworth's knee, which suprises me somewhat.

"And she harps on unconscionably about the continuation of the line, and my duty to the family. In short, Miss Wellesley-Clegg, my life would be a d—d sight more peaceful if I gave in and became leg-shackled. What do you say, Miss Wellesley-Clegg?"

"You should kneel, Aylesley," the Mad Poet says.

He calls him *Aylesley*?

"I don't believe so, sir. This carpet is thick with dog hair and my valet would be most disappointed. You know how unpleasant he can become about the state of my clothes."

Aylesworth pats the Mad Poet's hand and sighs. "You are such a romantic, my dear."

"You mean—you mean you want to *marry* me?"

Aylesworth turns his attention back to me. "Why, yes, Miss Wellesley-Clegg. It's an excellent solution all round. I could keep you in bonnets, and I wouldn't be ashamed to have you on my arm in public, particularly if you follow my advice at the dressmaker's. And if there were, ah, consequences following your little adventure, my dear mama would be delighted. We'd be expected to continue the family line, but I daresay we could come to some arrangement."

I know I should say something to the effect that I am honored, but I am so surprised I can only stare at the pair of them, who are now staring at each other again.

"Thank you," I say eventually. "That's very kind of you, Aylesworth. And Mr. Carrotte, too. But I . . ."

"Oh, Lord." Aylesworth looks at me with pity. "Please do not tell me you harbor fond feelings for your seducer. How dreadfully unfashionable. Well, my dear, you may certainly continue your liaison with my—our, that is—blessing. Is that one of your aunt's gowns you are wearing?"

I nod. Aylesworth gestures to me to stand and flicks away the fichu at my neckline. "Hideous," he murmurs, and produces a small pocketknife. "This trim is a disgrace. If I may, Miss Wellesley-Clegg?"

As he removes the braid around the neckline and sleeves of the dress, I consider his offer. I should certainly be one of the best-dressed ladies in town, and would have a free rein at the dressmaker's. And, from the sound of it, a free rein in just about any sphere I chose.

Aylesworth, having finished removing the trim, undoes the ribbon holding my Grecian knot and fusses with my hair. "Capital hair, wouldn't you agree, Carrotte? Almost as handsome as yours. You should cut it, Miss Wellesley-Clegg, and then I could have a matched pair."

I catch a glance of myself in the mirror and am most impressed by what he has done with my hair—Hen herself could not do so good a job. "Sir, I have no doubt I should be the best-dressed woman in town, but I am afraid it would not suit. Surely you can see I want more. I should not be happy, although I am most honored that you thought of me."

"Ah, well." Aylesworth reties the ribbon. "A pity indeed, Miss Wellesley-Clegg, for it's not every woman to whom I'd make an offer."

He bows, Carrotte bows, and I curtsey. We are tremendously polite, and were I not so weary with sadness I should be excited at having received such a worldly and wicked proposal. But I do feel a little better, and certainly less of a frump in my aunt's gown, and my hair has never looked better. Why, if I had accepted Aylesworth's proposal I should hardly need a maid, for my husband could have served as such.

The two gentlemen leave shortly after, arm in arm, and Aunt Rowbotham bustles me upstairs again to her bedchamber. She has me sort her stockings, and I foresee hours of darning in my near future.

"Aunt, I believe Roland would like to go for a walk."

As I say the word, Roland pants and his eyes protrude further from his head in excitement.

"The footman can take him." She reaches for the bell-pull.

"Oh, Aunt, I should so like some fresh air. I'll take him into the garden."

Roland grunts and cavorts heavily around me.

"Very well." She does not sound displeased, but sends a footman for a leash, and finally I am able to descend the stone steps into the garden. It is pleasant to get outside, the only drawback being that I am in the company of Roland, cross-eyed, snorting, and intent on giving every plant some male attention.

I haul him down through the flowerbeds, past the kitchen garden and chickens, and to my delight find the door that leads into the alley unlocked. I slip out. A few servants linger here, the men smoking and flirting with the women, and they're too interested in each other's company to take much notice of me. And so I set off for my sister's house. It is closest to Aunt Rowbotham's, and in truth I am afraid to go home—or what used to be my home, before I became a Fallen Woman. I know my aunt would have admitted Mama and Papa if they had called, and I fear I am cast off from my family. I cannot bear the thought that I might be turned away.

Roland is quite out of breath, his tongue drooling from his mouth when we arrive. To my relief, the butler admits me, but leaves me standing in the hall, where Roland sits on the marble, wheezing and grunting, and it is there my sister finds us.

She is accompanied by a footman. Oh, how degrading. She will use force to eject me from her house!

The footman looks embarrassed. He coughs, and murmurs, "Beg your pardon, miss, Mrs. Pullen can't talk to you."

"Oh, dear."

"Yes, miss, Mr. Pullen has forbidden it."

Diana beckons him over and they confer, whispering together. Then he crosses the hall to me.

"Mrs. Pullen likes the way you have done your hair, miss, and wants to know whether you would like to take tea."

"Oh, yes, thank you, and a bowl of water for Roland, if she would be so kind." At least if I drink tea with her, she may unbend a little. "May I enquire how her health is? And that of Master James?"

"Oh, he's a right little rascal, miss. Beg your pardon, Mrs. Pullen." He crosses to her side to receive her official answer.

This is absurd! Why, with the black-and-white tile patterns of the hall, and the to-and-fro motion of the footman, it is though we are participants in a game of chess. I take a step forward, just at the moment the butler, who peers out at the street from the small window by the front door, announces that Pullen has returned home.

My sister looks at me in horror and shakes her head.

I gather Roland to my bosom—he is quite heavy and smells horrible, and pants into my face—and run upstairs.

There is only one place to go, one person who can save me—it has come to me in a flash. Why, oh why, have I not seen his worth before? Why did I allow myself to be seduced—or almost seduced, or as good as, and what a pity I shall never have the pleasure of being seduced properly, or improperly I should say—by that most vile rake who has abandoned me? Dear Tom, who has always been my friend, even when I least deserved it, and who now will probably not chase me with wriggling worms.

I burst into his office. He starts, and rises to his feet, knocking over a cup of tea on his desk, soaking the papers lying there.

"Oh, Tom, Tom," I cry. "You are my only hope. My family have disowned me. Please help me! I'll do anything you want!" And I fly into his arms.

Chapter 25

Miss Wellesley-Clegg

Of course I had forgotten about Roland, who does not seem too happy to find himself crushed between us, and I swear, becomes even more odiferous. That, and a certain stillness about Tom make me back away.

"*Anything*?" he repeats. He produces a handkerchief and blots the mess on his desk.

Good heavens, I really did say that. "Yes. Anything." To cover my extreme embarrassment I put Roland onto the floor, where he slurps up spilled tea.

"You asked me quite recently not to propose marriage to you." He folds his arms and glares at me, as though he was angry with me, and I cannot bear it.

"Tom, please—"

"Miss Wellesley-Clegg, I am not a—a piece of clothing, a bonnet or some such that you can take from a peg on the wall when you fancy a change, or when you have need of me." This is so close to my own heartless assessment of Tom that tears of shame rise to my eyes. "I have feelings, too, Miss Wellesley-Clegg, but there's only so much a man can take. You broke my heart once, and I won't let you do it again."

"I—I'm sorry."

"And I certainly can't afford to keep a mistress."

Well, I asked for that. We speak plainly where we come from.

"Philly," he says then, more gently than I expected, which makes me cry harder, "you don't love me the way I love you. You never will. You're asking to make yourself unhappy, and me along with you. It's no good, lass."

I have to acknowledge he is right. I have never been so ashamed in my life, not even when I speculate on what vulgarities I may have uttered in the church in front of the *ton*. "Forgive me," I say, and wipe my nose on my sleeve.

"I'll escort you back to your aunt's," he says.

"No, Tom. You don't have to do that. Pullen would be angry if he found out. I have Roland to protect me if you could call a hackney."

He nods and accompanies me downstairs. Pullen, fortunately, is nowhere in sight, and neither is my sister.

We wait together in silence as a footman is sent to summon a hackney, and then Tom accompanies me outside. His silence almost breaks my heart. I have lost a dear friend through my own selfishness.

"Tom," I say, as I step into the carriage, "I should like to ask you something I have wondered about for years. Do you remember when I fell in the duck pond when I was five?"

He nods, smiling slightly.

"Did you push me in?"

Then he leans forward and kisses my cheek. "Not telling," he whispers, shuts the carriage door, and I am driven away.

Roland, exhausted by the exciting events of the day, snores horribly on the short journey back to Aunt Rowbotham's. By this time it is almost dark, and after I have paid the driver and I am about to ascend the steps to the house, a cloaked figure dashes toward me. Heavens, it is a brigand! Or a thief! I scream quite loudly, and Roland, growling horribly, lurches forward, teeth bared.

I am afraid he will catch something if he bites the ruffian, and haul him into the house, telling him that even though he stinks he is the best and bravest of dogs.

The butler takes my cloak and bonnet and tells me, to my surprise, that my aunt expects me in the drawing-room. She is not there, but someone else is—my dear papa.

He holds out his arms to me and I burst into tears once more.

"There, there, lass," he says. "Don't take on. Everything's all right."

It is not, but I am grateful to him for saying it.

"How is Mama?" I ask.

He shakes his head. "Silent as the grave."

We both sit down and he hands me a large handkerchief. "I owe you an apology, lass."

It's the last thing I expect to hear, and I stop crying from surprise.

"You see," he continues, "I laid a trap for Blackwater, but I wasn't quite clever enough. I baited him with the fifty guineas—I knew as soon as I was out of the house, or supposedly so, he'd ask you for money. And I knew he'd press you to marry him while I was gone. But I had to catch him red-handed, although I never intended it to happen at the altar. I meant to confront him at the house, but there was some problem with traffic—a dray overturned from some fool driving a hackney too fast, apparently."

"Why didn't you tell me?" I burst into tears anew. "Did you trust me so little?"

He doesn't answer, but I know what he is thinking, and I don't like it one bit. His daughter was frivolous enough to be almost engaged to two gentlemen at once and made a dreadful mistake. And I have spent a huge amount of Papa's money on bonnets. I shall not buy one for at least two months. After one month I shall allow myself to look in the windows of milliners' shops, but only look. I shall not go inside . . . "I'm sorry," I whisper. "Papa, is it true that he runs Mrs. Bright's house?"

Papa gazes at me without speaking for a long, uncomfortable moment. "It is. Your young man—the young man before last, that is, wrote me a letter that went to Lancashire and back telling me about the captain—and he's an impostor with the regiment, too. And then this young woman was brave enough to come forward."

I realize then, that in my pleasure at seeing my father, I had not noticed a woman who sits quietly to one side in a dark corner of the room.

She rises and curtsies. At first I barely recognize her with clothes on, or by the bruises which distort her pretty face.

"Why, Kate!" I say. "Kate, what has happened to you?"

"He did it, miss. That captain. He was boasting in Mrs. Bright's house how he had an heiress madly in love with him, and let slip your name. So I went to find your father." She stares at her hands. "I don't read too well, miss. So it took me a time to find where you lived, even though you gave me your papa's card, and the first time I went they told me he wasn't home."

I sit beside her and take her hand. "When did he beat you, Kate?"

"After the wedding—I mean the—you know, in the church. I went back to the house, hoping to gather my clothes and leave, but he caught me." She smiles, but with a distinct wobble in her chin. "Twopence ha'penny's too much, miss. He's more of a penny three farthings."

"Papa, I should like to hire Kate as my maid," I say, wondering if I even have an allowance anymore. "That is, Kate, if you'd like to have the position."

"Good girl," Papa says. "And now, what's to do about Mr. Linsley? I presume it is he? He has to marry you, lass, whatever his family may say."

"That wastrel?" Aunt Rowbotham thunders into the room. "You'll take tea, I trust, brother? Why, my footman has turned him away three times already today, and he brings shame upon the street, waiting in a hackney outside all day. I have twice asked the Watch to send him on his way. She cannot marry Linsley. He keeps an actress as mistress and has half a dozen b—s from all I hear."

"Only one," I say, "and he is a very sweet baby, Aunt. And why did you turn Inigo away?" I realize then that the brigand outside the house must have been Inigo—and I nearly let Roland bite him!

She snorts. "Nonsense, miss. Babies make messes, particularly if they're boys, and you don't want anything to do with that reprobate Linsley. Brother, I'll take Philomena on as my companion, and she shall play cribbage and read to me and take Roland for walks, and be cosy with no men in sight."

The thought of this, as grateful as I am, makes me sink back on the sofa in horror.

Aunt Rowbotham pours tea and offers biscuits, first to Roland and then to us.

"Mr. Linsley is obliged to marry her, if what she said in the church is true," Papa says. "Is it, Philly?"

"Well, yes, but Mrs. Gibbons was in bed with us too . . ."

Papa sprays tea over himself. Kate looks at me with new respect in her eyes.

"No, no, it wasn't like that." I slap Papa's back as he chokes and splutters.

"Well," he says after he has recovered, "his brother forbade him to marry you and they threaten to disown him if he disobeys. And you see, Philly, I don't know whether Mr. Linsley, as pleasant a young man he is, has the courage to withstand them. He's much attached to his family, for all their pride and faults."

"Then why has he called here three times today?"

After an uncomfortable silence, Kate speaks. "Well, miss, you see, he's packed his mistress off to the country, and is maybe on the lookout for one in town. His family wouldn't object to that, I'd wager. That's what the girls at Mrs. Bright's say, anyway, and we're usually right about men."

"That's monstrous!" I spring to my feet and burst into tears again. My biscuit falls from my saucer and Roland waddles over to slurp it from the carpet.

The doorbell rings very loudly at this point, and I look out of the window to see Inigo there.

It is too much. I recall what I said in the church, my shameful public admission, my treatment of Tom Darrowby, and now the dreadful doubts planted in my head.

Maybe he did only do it for Weaselcopse. Maybe he was only interested in my fortune, and now that is gone—for Papa has not said he'll cut me off without a penny, but he may yet do so—my person and the tattered remnants of my honor are all that remain.

I bolt out of the drawing room as the footman opens the front door and look around for shelter.

There is only one place to go.

I slam the door shut, bolt it, and curl up on the wooden seat.

"I know she's here," I hear Inigo shout. "Let me in, damn you."

I believe at this point Papa, Aunt Rowbotham, and Kate emerge from the drawing room. Roland, too, as a series of yips and snarls, in conjunction with colorful language from Inigo, suggests he has joined the fray.

Papa shouts something about a horsewhip and restoring his daughter's honor. My mild-mannered papa! I am proud of him.

Aunt Rowbotham announces that men are not welcome in her house, particularly Inigo.

"Philomena!"

Oh, I will not listen to him. I cover my ears.

I cannot become his mistress. I have to marry, but no one will have me now, unless Papa packs me off to marry a mill-owner at home. Oh, horror!

The door shakes under a series of heavy blows. "Philomena, you ninny, open the door!"

I gather what little is left of my dignity. "Certainly not, sir." My voice shakes. "It is very ungentlemanly of you."

"What are you doing in there?"

"It's a water closet. What sort of question is that?"

"Well, hurry up. I want to propose to you." He thumps on the door again and mutters something about women taking so long in there, it must be all the petticoats.

My papa comments that he's always thought it so, too.

"Propose what?"

"Don't be obtuse, girl. Open up."

"No! Go away."

"D—n."

I can hear a sort of scratching, metallic sound. "Mr. Linsley?"

"Yes, Miss Wellesley-Clegg?"

"What are you doing?"

"Taking the door off its hinges. Your aunt's butler was good enough to lend me a screwdriver."

"Please stop."

"No."

"At least, send everyone else away."

I hear him walk away, presumably to confer with the others, and I try the door. It wobbles. I unbolt it and open it a crack to see what is going on.

"Philomena!" Inigo rushes inside, bearing me onto the wooden seat. "Marry me. Make me the happiest of men. I love you, you ninny."

I am so glad to see him, so very glad. He has shaved and looks as handsome as ever, and even while I protest I put my arms around him. "But your family—"

"Oh, don't worry about them. They've disowned me."

"What!" Oh, poor Inigo.

He doesn't seem unduly upset. "You see, I have no recourse now but to marry an heiress and satisfy the gossip-mongers. Say yes, Philomena."

"Inigo, how can we tell our children you proposed to me in a water-closet, twice, and each time I accepted you?"

"You forget the time I proposed to you in my former mistress's bed. Of course, you are quite right." He stands and straightens out the door, which now tilts at a crazy angle; only the bottom seems to be fastened securely. "After you, Miss Wellesley-Clegg."

Outside, he reaches into his coat pocket, removes a screwdriver, and sets the door into position. "Miss Wellesley-Clegg, make me the happiest of men. Put your hand into my pocket and hand me a screw."

I do so.

"Miss Wellesley-Clegg!"

"Yes, Mr. Linsley?"

"Philomena, for God's sake." He looks quite shocked and wild-eyed, to my delight. Now it is he, the rake, who is thrown all out of sorts.

I move my hand around in his trouser pocket. Goodness, it is most interesting!

"I didn't mean that pocket!" he hisses.

"Oh, I do beg your pardon." I put my other hand into the trouser pocket on the other side, thus neatly trapping him against me.

"Come on, Philomena. Behave yourself. Say you'll marry me, for God's sake."

"Are you not forgetting something, sir?"

"What?" He looks excessively distracted now.

"Aren't you supposed to tell me you love me?"

"I should think, Miss Wellesley-Clegg, that the answer lies at your fingertips."

"How very vulgar of you, Mr. Linsley. Nevertheless, I love you to distraction."

His lips brush against my hair, and it is the most natural thing for us in the world to kiss. "And I love you too. Marry me," he whispers. "You may put your hands in my pockets as much as you like, and you can buy bonnets to your heart's content."

What woman alive could refuse such a proposal?

Not I.

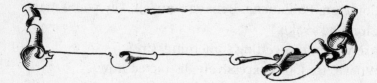

Letter from Miss Lydia
(or possibly Miss Charlotte)
Wellesley-Clegg

From the Great Northern Road, near L–

Dear Mama and Papa and my dearest sister,

The journey has been most interesting so far. We have seen several picturesque ruins and I have made some sketches. There are some very fine views hereabouts and we go often on walks and picnic. You will be interested to know that we visited the house of the Duke of P–, His Grace not being in residence, and saw many fine works of art. The house is reputed to have thirty bedchambers!

Phillie gave me a new ribbon for my bridesmaid's bonnet, but I liked it better the way before.

The weather continues fine and we are all well.

I send my love to you all and to Hen, and I hope the house in Lancashire still stands.

Your most loving daughter and sister,

Char Wes Blye

Sister,

I trust you managed to secrete this note away as we agreed upon, for I have much to tell you that I do not think Papa and Mama should know about. To think you and I quarreled so violently on who was to accompany Mr. and Mrs. Linsley on their honeymoon! It is, as Papa promised, an educational experience, but possibly not in the way he meant.

As usual, I am in the parlor of an inn in the middle of nowhere and it is pouring with rain. Kate is darning yet another tear in Philomena's nightrail—I did not realize the amount of damage done to linen on a honeymoon, although she shrugs and says Mr. Linsley is a passionate man. He and our sister are of course in their bedchamber, where they retired shortly after breakfast, she saying she needed to put on a different bonnet, and he, with a foolish grin on his face, saying he would help her. They have been there some four hours. So it is, most of the time.

The day before yesterday, when it did not rain, we went out to see some druidical ruin or some such (a collection of large stones in a field where cows were much in evidence—my new boots are quite ruined, I fear), and Phillie and Mr. Linsley wandered off. I was quite worried that they were lost, but eventually they reappeared, both of them grinning stupidly, much disarranged, and with twigs in their hair.

When we visited the Duke of P—'s house I regret that the housekeeper who showed us around thought Phillie and I were relations of Wellington and was most obsequious. Naturally Mr. and Mrs. Linsley became separated from us for some time and I suspect they visited at least one of His Grace's thirty bedchambers. However, I enjoyed the house greatly. There was a magnificent gallery of statues, many of gentlemen in the classical style, i.e. unclothed, and I shall show you my sketches on our return. Tomorrow we

[Author's note: At this point the original letter is overwritten in another, barely-readable hand. Since the words stockings and pins are legible, we can only assume the letter was recycled into yet another Wellesley-Clegg shopping list.]

A+

AUTHOR INSIGHTS, EXTRAS, & MORE...

FROM
JANET MULLANY

AND
AVON A

> "Look here, I have bought this bonnet. I do not think it is very pretty; but I thought I might as well buy it as not. I shall pull it to pieces as soon as I get home, and see if I can make it up any better."
>
> And when her sisters abused it as ugly, she added, with perfect unconcern, "Oh! but there were two or three much uglier in the shop; and when I have bought some prettier coloured satin to trim it with fresh, I think it will be very tolerable."
>
> **Jane Austen, *Pride and Prejudice***

I started writing Philomena and Inigo's story after finishing a manuscript so full of gloom, doom, and drama that even the weather was spectacularly bad. *The Rules of Gentility* was light relief, based very loosely on *Bridget Jones's Diary* but without daily weigh-ins or cigarette and calorie counts (for which, I admit, I could not find any Regency equivalent). Although I started it for my own entertainment, poking gentle fun at both romantic historical fiction and chicklit, somehow, frighteningly, it took on a life of its own. It was also a joke on me, since I'd sworn, in public, that I'd never, *ever* write about a nineteen-year-old virgin prancing about in drawing-rooms.

Oops.

I realized that despite my cavalier attitude a book was writing itself and it deserved some attention from me. I was also creating yet another version of the Regencyland beloved by readers and writers of historical romance—a world of very selective history (as is all historical fiction, romance or otherwise), where certain beloved myths were trotted out again and again.

So what was my new Regencyland?

I kept going back to Lydia Bennett and her bonnets.

What if . . . those magic words are a writer's springboard.

What if my heroine was a woman of no particular talent or ambition, other than the perfectly acceptable one (for the times) of wanting to make a good marriage? What if her abiding passion was fashion—she had the wealth to purchase a large number of bonnets and the leisure to pick them apart and rework them.

This raised another question—was there enough here to create a story? Yes—so long as I wrote it from the deepest point of view possible (yeah, it's a writer thing), getting right inside Philomena's head—hence the use of first person. I also wanted to provide enough distance for the reader to laugh *at* her as well as *with* her (you're allowed). And I thought it might be a good idea to give Inigo's perspective, too, because we all like the idea of inhabiting a man's head, in fiction, and on a temporary basis. Besides, it was more interesting for me that way, and, remember, this was initially all about *my* entertainment.

Naturally, my own Regencyland (doom, gloom, bad weather) crept in—some of the grit beneath the glamour, with characters who aren't quite *ton* (like Philomena herself) and some, servants and actors, who definitely aren't. I also explored, to a somewhat fluffy extent, the role families played then. One of my smart critique partners, Kate Dolan, pointed out that although we're used to the notion that women had little choice then, men didn't either—they did what they were told and pursued the profession their family chose. Duty was the order of the day. You did what your family told you to; if you made your bed, you lay on it. And, happily for the writer, those families can be as dysfunctional as any guests on the *Jerry Springer Show*.

However, as Jane Austen herself said, "let other pens dwell on guilt and misery." Here are some of my favorite Regencyland myths, in the form of the Top Ten things no one would ever say in a Regency-set historical romance.

The heroine:

1. Hell with Almack's. I think I'll stay home and entertain myself with the footmen.

2. I might as well marry the first man who offers for me. I can always have passionate love affairs afterward.

3. I never really wanted to be a writer/surgeon/spy/scientist/explorer/archaeologist/herbalist/highwayperson/governess/publisher/artist/balloonist/acrobat/pirate/opera singer/engineer. It just seemed to make me more attractive to eligible men.

4. Oh, Papa, what a shame you gambled away the family fortune. I'm afraid I can't think of anything I could possibly do to help out.

5. A devastatingly handsome, notorious, wicked rake? Eeeew.

6. I know it's our wedding night, but would you mind terribly if I got on with my knitting?

7. I don't care if that adorable lisping child is the apple of the hero's eye. If she doesn't shut up I'll slap her.

8. Pay no attention to my siblings. They're only here for the sequels.

9. Would you mind using one of those things made from animal intestines?

10. You don't have any? Look in my reticule.

The hero:

1. No brandy for me, thank you. It gives me terrible wind.

2. But I *always* wear a nightshirt and nightcap. Why should it be any different tonight?

3. Butler, remove this strange woman from my bed immediately.

4. All this striding around is giving me groin injuries.

5. No, no. I insist, madam. You take the floor. I'll be quite comfortable in this huge bed.

6. Send my valet for some Rogaine. I have been indulging in overmuch hair raking.

7. I'm afraid some women have complained it's rather on the small side.

8. I am Everard Dominic Benedict Ashford Alexander Artichoke FitzGrennan, Duke of Hawkraven, known and feared as Satan's Elbow, but you may address me as . . . Cuddles.

9. I really don't want to go to a gambling hell tonight. Couldn't we just stay home and read up on the bills we're supposed to vote on tomorrow in the House?

10. Waterloo? Oh, it was quite fun, actually.

Janet Mullany

JANET MULLANY's debut novel was a Signet Regency, _Dedication_ (2005), that went on to win several awards including the 2006 Golden Leaf. She was raised by half of an amateur string quartet in England, and was persecuted from an early age for reading too long in the family's only bathroom. After discovering Georgette Heyer, she spent many happy hours exploring the city of Bath and longing to be transported back in time, although worried about how she'd explain the miniskirt. Now living near Washington, D.C., she has worked as an archaeologist, draftsperson, classical music radio announcer, opera publicist, and editorial assistant at a small press. Janet also writes erotic historicals under the pseudonym of Jane Lockwood. Find out more at www.janetmullany.com.